"Do You Hate Me Now As You Did Before?"

Megan asked. Helplessly Daniel shook his head. "What do you feel this minute?" she persisted. "Tell me."

"I don't need to tell you. A woman who's been pursued by so many men must know desire when she sees it."

"Perhaps," she murmured.

"Does that please you, Megan? Is that what you really want, to make me your slave? You're determined to make me say I want you—"

"I don't need to hear you say it," she reminded him.

"That's right. I gave myself away last night. Just how far into the net do you want to lure me?"

"Why don't you try and find out?"

Dear Reader,

Just when you thought Mother Nature had turned up the heat, along comes Silhouette Desire to make things even *hotter*. It's June...the days are longer, the kids are out of school, and we've got the very best that romance has to offer.

Let's start with our *Man of the Month, Haven's Call,* which is by Robin Elliott, a writer many of you have written to tell me is one of your favorites.

Next, we have *Salty and Felicia* by Lass Small. If you've ever wondered how those two older Browns got together, well, now you'll get to find out! From Jennifer Greene comes the latest installment in her JOCK'S BOYS series, *Bewildered*. And Suzanne Simms's series, HAZARDS, INC., continues with *The Pirate Princess*.

Anne Marie Winston has created a tender, wonderful story, *Substitute Wife*. And if you like drama and intensity with your romance, don't miss Lucy Gordon's *Uncaged!*

It just doesn't get any better than this...so read and enjoy.

All the best,

Lucia Macro
Senior Editor

Please address questions and book requests to:
Reader Service
U.S.: P.O. Box 1325, Buffalo, NY 14269
Canadian: P.O. Box 1050, Niagara Falls, Ont. L2E 7G7

LUCY GORDON
UNCAGED

SILHOUETTE *Desire*®
Published by Silhouette Books
America's Publisher of Contemporary Romance

SILHOUETTE BOOKS

ISBN 0-373-05864-0

UNCAGED

Printed in U.S.A.

LUCY GORDON

met her husband-to-be in Venice, fell in love the first evening and got engaged two days later. They're still happily married and now live in England with their three dogs. For twelve years Lucy was a writer for an English women's magazine. She interviewed many of the world's most interesting men, including Warren Beatty, Richard Chamberlain, Roger Moore, Sir Alec Guinness and Sir John Gielgud.

In 1985 she won the *Romantic Times* Reviewer's Choice Award for Outstanding Series Romance Author. She also won a Golden Leaf Award from the New Jersey Chapter of the RWA, was a finalist in the RWA Golden Medallion contest in 1988 and won the 1990 Rita award in the Best Traditional Romance category for *Song of the Lorelei*.

Prologue

"Megan Elizabeth Anderson, you have been found guilty of the shocking crime of murder. Have you anything to say before sentence is passed?"

The woman in the dock lifted her head. After three months in prison she was still beautiful. If anything, the way her hair was pulled back accentuated her fine bone structure with its high cheekbones and the hollows beneath. Even without makeup, it was still a lovely face, although the dark shadows under her eyes hinted at sleepless nights.

Some of the public who'd crowded in on this last day of her trial had heard of her. Once she'd been a top model, but she'd given it up when she'd become a mother, and settled into a life of domesticity with her son and her businessman husband. She'd seemed the woman with everything—money, a delightful child and a perfect marriage. But the marriage had broken up a year ago, and now she was on trial for murder.

Some of them noticed that Brian Anderson wasn't there now. Despite their separation, he'd sat through every day of the trial as the evidence piled up against his estranged wife, but he obviously hadn't been able to face this last day with its inevitable verdict. The onlookers wondered what she felt about his desertion, but no one could tell. After the first glance at his empty place, she'd averted her gaze and never looked again. A cool customer, they said.

One man who'd made sure of being present was Detective Inspector Daniel Keller, the policeman who'd made the case against her. He'd given his evidence in a hard, expressionless voice, and taken his place in the body of the court. He was here now for the verdict. He was in his early thirties, with a face that might have been handsome, except that something had happened to it. It was as though he'd fitted a cage over his features, a cage made of harshness and grim determination that had subtly reshaped every line, crushing out human vulnerability. He didn't look at Megan Anderson, but stared into the distance. He was deathly pale and seemed strung up with tension, as though only an almighty effort of nerves kept him going. Eerily, the prisoner wore exactly the same expression.

"Have you anything to say?" the judge repeated.

Megan Anderson took a step forward and gripped the edge of the dock. "I've only one thing to say," she declared in a voice that rang around the courtroom. "And that's what I've said from the start, and what I'll say until my dying day. I am innocent of murder. As for those who falsely put me here, *may God forgive them, because I never will!*"

At last something seemed to reach Detective Inspector Keller. He looked at her sharply, as though his head had been wrenched around by force. No one doubted that her words were meant for him. She was looking at him with hate, and now the spectators had no doubt that she was a murderess, because if she could have struck him dead she would have done so. He returned her gaze with harsh stoicism. For a moment, the bitter, jagged atmosphere between them was stronger than anything else in the courtroom.

Even the judge was taken aback, but he recovered himself and addressed the prisoner again. "You will do yourself no good by these outbursts," he told her severely. "You've made your allegations and the jury has rejected them and found you guilty of murder—rightly, in my opinion. I have no choice but to sentence you to imprisonment for the rest of your life."

An hour later Megan Anderson was sitting in a van with black sides and high barred windows, on her way to start a life sentence in prison. At the same moment Detective Inspector Keller was locked in his bedroom with a bottle of whiskey, determinedly seeking oblivion.

One

"**F**rankly, I think you've been very lucky," the policewoman said.

Megan stared at her. "Lucky? I was imprisoned for a murder I didn't commit, and after stealing three years of my life they finally admit they were wrong, and you say I'm *lucky?*"

The policewoman gave her a hard look. "If you listened carefully to what the appeal court judges said, they didn't actually admit they were wrong. You got off on a technicality."

"Oh, yes, a technicality." Megan seethed. "They discovered that there was a witness to my alibi all the time, but a corrupt policeman had suppressed it. You call that a technicality?"

Before her tormentor could answer, the door opened and Janice Baines, Megan's lawyer, came in. They were in an anteroom of the court, where three appeal judges had just ordered Megan's release. She'd arrived in a prison van, but she would leave in Janice's car a free woman—whatever that might mean.

"There's a crowd outside," Janice observed. "A lot of them are journalists."

"I'm not talking to journalists," Megan insisted. "I just want to be left alone."

"That's a good line," the policewoman said cynically. "You can sell your story for twice the price if you play hard to get."

"Get me out of here, Janice," Megan said bitterly, "before I commit a real murder."

"My car's around the back," Janice said, taking her arm and steering her out into the corridor.

There were a couple of journalists covering the rear entrance, and they made a dash when they saw Megan. She managed to get in the car and slam the door, but they hammered on the roof, shouting questions, and one of them pressed a checkbook against the window. Luckily Janice was a skilled driver, and in seconds they'd left the pack behind.

"She as good as said I was guilty," Megan said furiously. "A technicality, my God!"

"Look, I don't want to spoil your day of triumph," Janice said after a moment, "but I'm your lawyer, and I have to give you the facts. I'd have been happier if they'd given you a ringing endorsement of innocence."

"But there was a witness who said he saw me miles away at the moment Henry Grainger was killed," Megan said wildly.

"Not quite," Janice interrupted. "In his statement he said he saw a woman who answered your general description, but it was too dark for him to make out details. If he'd appeared at your original trial, the jury might easily have decided that it didn't prove anything. The appeal court released you today because Detective Inspector Keller concealed the statement instead of giving it to the defense, as he should have done. I hate to be brutal, Megan, but it *was* a technicality, and that's going to affect what happens now."

There was a silence before Megan said, "I saw Brian's lawyer in court."

"Yes, I talked to him before I collected you. I'm afraid he said that nothing's changed. Brian still thinks you're guilty, and he's not going to give Tommy back to you. He won't even let you see him."

"Oh, God." Megan's words were almost a scream as she buried her head in her hands and sat shaking.

Janice gave her a sympathetic glance before returning her attention to the road. "We'll fight it," she said. "Don't despair yet."

Megan raised her head abruptly. She was calm again. "I'm not despairing," she said. "If I didn't give way to despair during three years in that place, I'm not going to do it now."

"That's the spirit."

"Frankly, I think you've been very lucky," Detective Chief Inspector Masters said.

Daniel Keller stared at him. "Lucky? I'm being kicked off the force and you say I'm *lucky?*"

"You're lucky to have only been suspended on paid leave. You *haven't* been kicked off the force, although if I had my way you would have been."

"Oh, yes," Daniel said. "It's no secret that you've been looking for ways to get rid of me ever since you came here two years ago."

"I don't like mavericks, Keller. I don't like loners. I don't like officers who undermine my authority by tossing the book aside whenever it suits them, or officers who suppress evidence *and then get caught.* I don't like seeing a murderess go free because one of my men fouled up. It's a black mark against this station."

It's a black mark against your *possible promotion,* Daniel thought. *That's what's really worrying you.* But all he said was, "Who says she's a murderess? The appeal court cleared her."

"Oh, no, they didn't. They very carefully stopped short of declaring her innocent, but because you cut corners they had to let her go. That makes me angry."

Masters was a red-faced, choleric man who seemed to be angered by everything in sight. But in particular he was infuriated by the tall, rangily built man in the battered leather jacket and old jeans standing on the other side of his desk. Daniel Keller was in deep trouble, yet instead of looking chastened, he regarded his superior coolly, his lips twisted in an arrogant half smile that only just escaped being a jeer.

"It makes me angry," Masters repeated. "So do these headlines."

He waved an impatient hand at the newspapers on his desk. One headline read Suppression Of Evidence Leads To Release. Another, Why Did He Conceal Evidence? Witness Asks, Why Wasn't I Called To Testify?

"It's either incompetence or corruption, and I won't tolerate either," Masters snapped. "By rights you should be out of here for good, but I've had to listen to a lot of bleeding hearts stuff from your colleagues about how you were under strain from 'personal problems' at the time—although how that justifies fouling up, I don't know."

Daniel went rigid with distaste as his most painful wounds were casually flicked by this gross creature. "My problems were—and remain—my own affair," he said stiffly. "I never asked for allowances to be made for me on that account."

"So I should think. Clear your desk and go. And don't come back until you're sent for."

"Which will be never if you have your way," Daniel said ironically.

"As you say."

When Daniel had gone, a genial, lazy-looking, middle-aged man pushed open a glass door to enter Masters's office. "That was a bit rough, wasn't it, Chief?" he asked. "They weren't just any old personal problems. His wife and son—"

"We all have things to bear, Canvey," Masters said without looking up. "Get back to your work."

Canvey retreated, but instead of returning to work he slipped downstairs and waylaid Daniel as he was leaving. "You'll be back," he said reassuringly. "Probably do you good to have a rest. It's a pity you didn't have one back then."

"Do you think she did it, Canvey?" Daniel asked slowly.

"'Course she did. This was just a technicality."

"I should hate to think I sent an innocent woman away. If only I could remember exactly what happened . . . but it's all so blurred in my head."

"You weren't yourself in those days. You should have taken some time off. I told you so at the time."

Daniel made his way out to his car, trying not to be conscious of the looks that followed him, some of them sympathetic, some full of barely concealed pleasure. His brusque manner, short fuse and unorthodox methods had made him many enemies, and not only among the criminal fraternity. Some of his so-called colleagues were glad to see him brought low. The thought made him lift his head still higher.

He groaned as he saw two men, one with a television camera, waiting for him. "I've got nothing to say," he told them firmly.

They followed him to his car, the reporter constantly trying to shove a microphone in front of him. "How do you feel about Megan Anderson's release?"

"I have no feelings about it one way or the other," he snapped. It was partly true. His feelings were in such turmoil that he couldn't sort them out.

"Is it true that the police are refusing to reopen the case?"

"Ask them."

"Does that mean you've been dismissed?"

Now he knew how a fox felt when the hounds were after it. It was a horrible experience. He managed to keep hold of his temper until he got in the car, but when the reporter banged on the window, he wound the glass down and said "Get...out...of...my way" with such slow, emphatic menace that the man blanched and backed off.

He reached his house without further incident, and noted with relief that the crowds of press who'd made it a nightmare the day before had disappeared. But as he got out of his car, a man, who seemed to be mending the road, suddenly straightened and blocked his path. "Have you got any statement to make, Inspector?"

Daniel took hold of the reporter's ear. "Yes, I have a statement," he said with deceptive mildness. "It's this. You have one second to get out before you feel my foot in your rear." He let go, and the man scuttled away.

When Janice had asked where she'd wanted to go, Megan's answer had been simple. "Somewhere I can hide."

The result was an obscure boarding house in a shabby part of London. She had one room that doubled as a bedroom and living room, a tiny kitchen, and a bathroom the size of a postage stamp. The apartment wasn't much bigger than her prison cell, which accorded with Megan's mood. She was free only in the most limited sense. Everything that had once formed her life had been stripped from her, including her good name, but most of all, her son. For the moment she could see no way of getting them back.

She called her ex-husband repeatedly that afternoon, but he wouldn't speak to her. His mother answered the phone at home, and at work his secretary had orders not to put her through. Between calls she sat and brooded in terrible bitterness.

Her thoughts were chaotic, but one thing stayed constant. The face of Daniel Keller was there all the time—hard, unyielding, judging her—so convinced that he was right that he'd twisted the case and destroyed her. His face was burned into her consciousness by her hatred of him. She watched the television news reports and caught the moment when the reporter asked how he felt about her release, and his reply. "I have no feelings about it one way or another."

"Of course you haven't," she flung at his face on-screen. "What's it to you?"

It was some slight comfort to learn that he'd been suspended, although she felt, cynically, that he would be allowed back when the dust had settled. It was her own future that had been blasted.

Her first night alone was tormented by nightmares and she awoke crying out. One of the other residents knocked on her door to ask if she was all right. After that she tried to catnap for short periods, fearful of rousing the house. So far no one seemed to have recognized her, and this was her only hope of peace.

It was early spring, not a green, enchanted spring promising hope and rebirth, but a sodden fag end of winter, where it rained and rained and rained. The endless cascades of water beat against her ill-fitting windows and seeped in through the cracks, making the room damp. And the noise sometimes made it hard to hear anything else.

On the evening of her fourth day, just as she'd finished dressing for bed, she thought she heard a knock outside. Yawning she made her way to the door, then hesitated. A sudden letup in the rain gave her the chance to hear the knock again. "Who is it?" she called cautiously.

"Mrs. Anderson?" A man's voice reached her from the other side of the door.

"If you're a journalist, go away."

"I'm not a journalist...." The man hesitated. "I'm Daniel Keller."

Sheer outrage made her pull open the door to confront him. "Get out of here!" she said fiercely. "How *dare* you come pestering me?" Her voice rose to a cry. *"Haven't you done enough?"*

He was already halfway in. "I have to talk to you," he said urgently.

"And I *don't* have to talk to you," she said bitterly. "This isn't like those times you had me in the police station and I had to talk to you whether I wanted to or not. I'm free now, free of that damned prison where you put me with your lies and your frame-up, and free of *you*. I can tell you to get out, and that's what I'm doing."

He hesitated, driven by desperation but unwilling to use force. Megan's sharp voice had attracted attention in the shabby little boarding house. Doors were opening, curious heads appearing. "Please let me in," he said urgently.

"I told you to get out of here." She tried pushing against the door but he pushed harder and managed to get right into the room. Megan backed away swiftly, as though afraid he might touch her. "What's the matter with you?" she snapped. "Don't you understand the word no? Oh, but of course you don't. How often did I say 'no' to you three years ago? No, I didn't murder Henry Grainger. No, I don't know who did. No, I'm not lying. No, no, *no*. And how much notice did you ever take? Not a bit because you were so sure you were right and it was just a question of wearing me down until I confessed. And when I refused to oblige, you framed me."

"I didn't—"

"Don't lie to me," she cried. "You lied before and your lies cost me three years of my life. *They cost me my son.*"

Without warning, her fury drained away. She seemed to have little physical strength left, only what her taut nerves could give her. She'd lived on nervous energy through the agonizing days of her appeal; now that she was free, the energy came and went, so that she roller-coasted between being high on adrenaline and being too weak to stand. Only a moment ago she'd been possessed by the strength of anger. Now she felt like a rag doll. "Why on earth did you come here?" she asked, sitting down tiredly.

Daniel hesitated. If she'd looked up at his face she would have seen that it was as tortured as her own. He'd been little more than thirty when they'd first clashed, but the years since then had scored themselves twice over on his features. He'd been to hell, just as she had. But she saw none of this.

"I came because I had to," he said. "I can't just leave things like this."

"Why? Because you've been suspended? I'd say that you'd come by your just deserts and things should be left *exactly* like that."

With her brown eyes blazing at him, he remembered that as a model she'd been called Tiger Lady. She was rumored to have a short fuse and an explosive temperament, which had counted against her at the trial.

He remembered his first sight of her, three years ago, glamorous in a silk evening dress and velvet cape, her face skillfully made up. She'd been working for an escort agency and had just returned from a date when he'd called to "ask a few questions" about the violent death of her landlord, Henry Grainger. He'd made a professional note of her extravagant beauty, but it hadn't moved him. His heart had died exactly two months, three weeks and two days earlier—the day his wife had been killed by a drunken driver.

If he'd felt anything about Megan's looks it was antagonism at the expensive trappings that showed them

off. The trappings were gone now. She wore no
makeup, and her face was pale. The glamorous clothes
were gone, too. Her plain cotton nightgown was
mended in a couple of places, and her feet were bare.
Yet an irreducible beauty remained. It was there in the
high cheekbones and curved mouth, in the large,
haunted eyes.

"Mrs. Anderson," he said at last, "I know you find
this hard to believe, but I swear I wasn't corrupt. I
didn't suppress evidence."

"Don't take me for a fool. You had a witness who'd
seen me ten miles away at the time Grainger was killed,
and you buried his statement because it would have
ruined your case. How lucky for you that the constable who took that statement left the force and went to
Australia. You must have thought everything was
working out wonderfully. Only he came back and
started asking awkward questions, and that was lucky
for *me* because you were exposed for the cheat you are.
The only thing that amazes me is that you contented
yourself with hiding the statement. Why not destroy it
while you had the chance? Or would that have been too
dangerous for you? I suppose you prefer your corruption to be nice and safe."

"Stop this," he said desperately. "I didn't hide the
statement because I didn't know about it."

She looked at him derisively. "You can do better
than that. Constable Dutton handed it to you himself."

"Maybe he did. I don't know. I only know that I
have no recollection of it."

"And I suppose you have no recollection of scrib-
bling something on it? It was your handwriting."

"Yes, but—"

"And the way it got conveniently lost—hidden away in a file belonging to another case. I suppose you have 'no recollection' of that, either?"

"None at all. When it was found in that file I was as amazed as anybody, I swear it."

She actually smiled with incredulity that he should try to fool her with such a feeble story. "I don't know why you came here, but you're wasting your time," she said firmly.

"I came because I have to know the truth."

"Has the truth suddenly become important to you after all this time?" she asked sarcastically. "What use is it to tell you the truth? You don't believe it when you hear it. You really came because you want me to confess, then you'd feel all right, wouldn't you? And the force might take you back."

"It wouldn't make me feel all right to know you're guilty," he said harshly. "That would mean I'd made my case so clumsily that a murderess was freed too soon. Did I do that? Or did I jail an innocent woman? Either way, it's just as bad."

"Your arrogance is beyond belief," she snapped. "'Just as bad'? It may make no difference to you which way it turns out, but what about me? I don't matter, do I? To you I'm just part of an academic exercise in finding out which way your guilt lies. But I'm not. I'm a human being, and you've ruined my life. I didn't kill anyone, but because *you* made it look as if I did, they took my son away. Because of you I can't get to see him, even now. If my ex-husband has his way, I'll never see him again, *and it's all because of you.*"

Her voice rose to a scream as her nerves finally snapped, and she flew at him. For three dreary years she'd longed to inflict on him a fraction of the pain he'd caused her, and now he was here. She lashed out blindly, striking, clawing at his face, driven by uncontrollable fury.

Daniel backed up, raising his hands as a shield. What he saw in her face appalled him. Through his job he was used to witnessing despair and misery, but this was worse. It was as though Megan was too demented with anguish to know what she did. Some instinct made him stop trying to push her away and pull her against him, tightening his arms around her so that she was trapped. "Let me go," she screamed.

"I will when you stop trying to attack me," he said, speaking breathlessly for she was still thrashing about. "I just want us to talk."

"The only words I want to say to you are words of hate," Megan snapped. "Is that clear enough?"

But she was too exhausted to keep it up. The roller coaster was at work again, carrying her to the peak of rage only to plunge her back down into the depths. Suddenly she went limp in his arms and started to shake, not with anger but with grief. Daniel felt the violent trembling of her body against his own and it went through him like a pain. He knew what it was like to suffer like that, to curse heaven in bitterness and misery, and realize that cursing changed nothing. The loved one had gone, and the world was still a dark, barren place to be endured.

Sounds were coming from her, not weeping, but a kind of half-gasping moan, like the keening of a distraught animal. And again his own experience showed him the answer. That sensation of being an animal, feeling the loss of one's young like an agony in the flesh. How well he knew it. He was a man with a bitter sense of irony, and it wasn't lost on him that, of all the world, he was the best placed to empathize with her, yet there was no one whose help she wanted less. But then irony fled and he felt nothing but an overwhelming desire to calm her storm of grief. "Megan," he pleaded. "Megan . . . let me help you. . . ."

She grew still and he thought he'd gotten through to her. "It's cold in here," he said. "Haven't you got a dressing gown? And something to put on your feet?"

"When you've gone, I'm going to bed," she said tiredly. "I wish you'd leave now. Just go, and I'll be all right."

He realized that he hadn't gotten through, after all. She was simply too tired to argue anymore. "How can I walk away and leave you like this?" he demanded.

"The same way you walked away and left me in prison. I'm not your problem." She pushed against him and he reluctantly freed her. "Please go."

"Look—"

"Go." She went to the door and pulled it open. "Go away now, and don't come back."

Her head was turned toward him, so she didn't see what was outside the door. She saw only the sudden look of tension on his face, and when she turned, it was too late. The little crowd of men and women surged into her room, all babbling at once and taking pictures, blinding them both with flashbulbs.

"Mrs. Anderson have you anything to say?"

" . . . I'm authorized to offer you."

" . . . exclusive . . ."

"Why aren't the police looking for someone else?"

"Your story . . . if you'd only—"

"Go away," she screamed. "Go away and leave me alone!"

Instead of leaving, they pressed in on her further, forcing her to back away from them. But she suddenly stopped and plunged forward between them, forcing them to part. By the time they'd recovered from their surprise, she was out the door and racing down the stairs toward the front door. They raced after her, baying like hounds in pursuit.

Daniel hesitated, torn between two opposing instincts. He wanted to intervene and get them off her track, but if they recognized him, they'd have an even better story, one that would make them pursue her even more mercilessly. At last he followed them down and out into the street and saw that Megan had vanished. The pack poured into their vehicles and tore off in pursuit. He gave them a moment to get clear before going to his own car. He didn't think he'd have far to look for her. She was bound to be hiding nearby.

But an hour of combing the streets produced nothing. He checked her apartment in case she'd returned, but all he found was a journalist who'd had the same idea and looked set to wait out the night.

Cursing, Daniel got back into his car and began the search again. But it was useless, and at last he had to face the fact that Megan had vanished into the pouring rain wearing only a thin nightgown and nothing on her feet.

TWO

Megan didn't stop running until she was out of breath. She clutched something nearby and stood there heaving, trying to fight off a pain in her side. Gradually her head cleared enough for her to realize that she was holding a tree. She looked around and found herself in a large park that seemed empty except for herself.

She was unfamiliar with this part of London and she didn't know where she was. She'd fled blindly, and now she had no memory of entering the park and no idea of how to get home. But the dreary little apartment had never been home, and now it wasn't even a refuge. They'd found it and would be watching for her return. Her feet were bruised and bleeding and she was shivering with cold. She wondered why she'd ever thought things would be better once she'd left jail. They were worse. She was as much a prisoner as ever, but now she was a prisoner on the run, with nowhere to go.

To her surprise she discovered she wasn't cold anymore. Heat was stealing pleasantly through her limbs and all over her body, although the icy rain was still pouring down, plastering her hair over her eyes. She brushed her hair back, but it was still hard to see through the curtain of water that surrounded her. She began to stumble about, seeking an exit, although what she would do when she found one she didn't know. The whole evening seemed like just a dream. She'd dreamed that her enemy had come to call, just as she was dreaming now that she could hear his voice through the lashing of the rain.

She came to another tree and stopped to rest against it. But something in the pattern of the knots seemed familiar, and she realized that it was the same tree as before. How long had she been wandering around in circles? She had no notion of time.

"Megan." The voice was there again in her dream, and Daniel Keller mysteriously appeared through the curtain of water. "Megan. Thank God, I found you."

She regarded him without hostility, but without interest. He was no more than a shadow in her overheated consciousness. "Go away," she said indifferently. "I'm fine, really I am."

He put his hand on her forehead and swore. "You're burning up with fever. Come on." He picked her up and ran with her in his arms to where he'd left his car. He almost threw her into the backseat, wrenched off his jacket and wrapped it around her before getting into the front and starting up.

As he drove, he used his car phone to call his doctor, who was also a good friend. "I need a home call urgently," he said. "Can you be there in ten minutes? Thanks."

Dr. Angela Lang was there before him. She stood by his front door, a reassuringly motherly figure, as Daniel hurried up the path with Megan in his arms. "Help me put her to bed," he grunted as he carried Megan inside and passed Dr. Lang on the stairs without waiting for a response.

In the guest room, he stripped off Megan's sodden nightgown and dried her fiercely. "Good grief!" Angela exclaimed in sudden shock. "Isn't she—?"

"Yes, she is," Daniel said urgently. "Never mind that. Do something for her feet while I try to stop her getting pneumonia."

"The best thing is if I get her admitted into the hospital—"

"No!" Daniel said explosively. "She's had enough of institutions and people staring at her. She needs peace and privacy."

"Daniel, are you mad? If you want to save your career, this woman is dynamite."

"I know that," he said through gritted teeth.

"So what the devil is she doing in your house, unconscious and naked?"

"You're right," he said quickly. "She needs something warm to wear."

"That wasn't what I—" But Daniel had vanished, returning a moment later with a pair of his own clean pajamas. Angela gave up arguing and tended to Megan's bleeding feet.

"She isn't going to get pneumonia, is she?" Daniel asked when Megan was dressed and wrapped up under an electric blanket.

"I don't think so. Probably just a feverish cold, but if she gets worse, call me at once. Are you a good nurse? She'll need a lot of attention at first."

"Don't worry," he said with bleak humor, "I've got nothing else to do."

The heat that had comforted Megan in the park had given way to violent shivering. She was burning up with fever, yet at the same time she was like ice. Somebody was piling blankets onto her, but it was no use. Aches and pains chased themselves through her limbs. She wanted to sleep but she felt too ill.

Then she was being raised to a sitting position and a mug was being pressed to her lips. "Drink this." She vaguely remembered the man's voice but she couldn't place it. "It's hot milk and whiskey, and it'll do you good," he added.

She obeyed, and took the tablets he gave her. But when she lay down she was still restless and began tossing about, throwing off the blankets. He piled them back onto her and she threw them off again. He seemed to have inexhaustible patience, because no matter how often it happened he was always there to push her back against the pillows and soothe her. She tried to fight him off, muttering, "I've got to...got to..."

Got to what? She didn't know. She only knew that some terrible problem was going unsolved while she lay here, and nobody else understood.

But it seemed that he did understand because he murmured, "It's all right. Everything's going to be all right. Just sleep and let me do the worrying."

After a while she stopped struggling and lay there, her hand in his.

Daniel stayed quite still until he was sure she'd fallen asleep, then he gently tucked her hand under the blanket. He rose and stood looking down at her flushed face on the pillow. The strain was smoothed away from it now, but the dark shadows around her eyes told the story of inner torment.

"What have I done?" he murmured. "Dear God, what have I done?"

In the limbo between sleeping and waking Megan found herself experiencing a new sensation. Suddenly there was nothing to worry about because someone was taking care of her, someone strong who could shoulder all her burdens until she could cope with them again herself.

That had last happened when she was a child. Her parents had died when she was only sixteen, after which she'd had to fend for herself. She'd capitalized on her height and slender beauty to become a model, and for a few years she'd been in the front rank.

Then she'd met Brian Anderson. At first she'd been charmed by him, but the charm had faded as she'd realized he'd had only one priority—success. He'd been an accountant in a high-profile firm, and he'd adored her because she was successful and well-known. He'd enjoyed being seen with a beautiful woman on his arm, but she'd gradually become convinced that his feelings went very little deeper than that. She'd been on the verge of breaking off the relationship when she'd found out she was pregnant.

She'd never even considered an abortion. She'd wanted her baby, and Brian's eagerness to marry her had warmed her heart again. Perhaps his child would make him see the world in less monetary terms. But it had had the opposite effect. Money and success became doubly important. He was furious when she'd abandoned her career because she couldn't bear to be apart from her adored little son.

When Tommy was a year old, Brian had broken away from his firm to start up on his own. Megan had been an asset to him, presiding over dinner parties where every detail was perfect, including her own impeccable appearance. But the socializing had meant nothing to her. The guests were invariably people who might be "useful" and afterward Brian would discuss them entirely in terms of their money and the business they might bring his way.

The gap between herself and her husband had yawned wider every day, but she'd made the best of it for Tommy's sake, and would have continued doing so, if Brian hadn't gone too far. Trying to land a hugely rich but personally repellent client, he'd instructed her to "be nice" to him.

"Just how 'nice' do you want me to be?" Megan had asked in an icy tone that should have warned him.

Brian had shrugged. "He's worth millions, he's got no family and his hobby is speculation. Work it out."

Their own physical relationship had been over for a year at that point, but it was still a shock to discover that he'd respected her so little that he could suggest such a thing. When Brian returned home from work that evening, he'd found Megan and Tommy gone.

He'd tried to starve her back to him, refusing to allow her a penny even for the child's upkeep. So she'd returned to work, taking the kind of low-ranking modeling jobs that would once have been beneath her, and supplementing her income with escort work. In comparison to the luxurious life-style she'd left, they were hard up, but she was happier than she'd been for a long time—until the sky had fallen on her.

In all those years there'd never been anyone to murmur "It's all right...let me do the worrying." But now someone had said it, and the words had given her ease.

She opened her eyes and found herself in a strange room. It was large and shabby but comfortable. It didn't surprise her that she recognized nothing. The events of the past few days had made the unfamiliar familiar, and the unexpected, the norm. She was hot and achy all over, and her head felt as if it was stuffed with cotton wool.

Then the door opened, and her enemy came in. She stared, aghast, and tried to pull herself upright in the bed, but lead weights pulled her back. "What are you doing here?" she demanded in a hoarse whisper.

"This is my home," Daniel told her. "I brought you here after I found you in the park."

"How dare you!" It was hard to sound angry when she could hardly speak.

"I had no choice, Megan. I couldn't take you back to that apartment. The press had it staked out."

"Not here. Anywhere but here," she croaked.

"If you think about it, you'll see that this is the best place. Who would ever think of looking for you with me?"

She started to cough and could do nothing until the fit had subsided. When it was over, she lay back, drained, and looked at him helplessly.

Daniel laid a gentle hand on her forehead. "You've got a feverish cold," he said. "You stay here until you're well."

"You've taken a lot for granted," she said hoarsely.

"What would you prefer, the hospital, where you'll be stared at?" She shook her head weakly, beyond speech. "Don't waste what little voice you've got left in abusing me," he advised. "The doctor left you something to take. I'll get breakfast and make you comfortable, then you must get some more sleep. The bathroom's next door. Put this on." He indicated a thick terry-cloth robe lying across a chair, and left the room.

As soon as she got out of bed, her head swam. It took ten minutes to get into the robe and out of the room. The bathroom mirror showed her looking haggard, with large, feverish eyes, but it had been a long time since she'd cared what she looked like. Almost subliminally she noticed that the room was exclusively male. There was shaving tackle and toothpaste, but no talcum powder, or anything else to suggest a woman.

She slowly made her way back to the bedroom, holding on to the wall, and was leaning against it to regain her breath when Daniel appeared with breakfast. "Let me help you," he said, setting down the tray and reaching for her.

Her eyes glittered at him. "Don't...touch...me...." she said in an emphatic whisper.

Reluctantly he let his hands fall to his sides and watched edgily as she tottered back to bed. After that, she seemed to have no more fight in her, accepting the tablets he offered without protest, eating some of the breakfast, falling asleep and staying that way for the rest of the day.

That afternoon Daniel called Canvey. His old colleague greeted him with cautious warmth, until he heard what Daniel wanted. Then he exploded with outrage and apprehension. "Are you out of your mind, man? Do you want me to be thrown off the force, as well?"

"I know it's a lot to ask," Daniel said urgently, "but nobody need suspect. Just for one night, and you can have them back in the morning."

"Masters will have my head on a plate if he finds out."

"He won't find out. Please, Canvey, I'm desperate."

In the end, Canvey gave in as he was bound to do, since he owed his life to Daniel. He arrived after work that evening with a parcel that he thrust into Daniel's hands with the words, "Have these ready when I call tomorrow morning, or we're both in big trouble."

Daniel went into the back room where he kept his audio-video equipment, the one luxury he allowed himself. He opened the parcel and found that Canvey hadn't let him down. Inside were cassettes, both audio and video, of his interviews with Megan, three years ago, plus all his own notebooks.

He spent the night duplicating everything, and had just managed to get the parcel packed up by the time Canvey called on his way to work the next day. After thanking Canvey, he made his way upstairs with Megan's breakfast. He found her coughing and sneezing, and unable to do much more than nibble on some toast. He put fresh sheets on the bed and helped her back in. She made no protest. In fact, she hardly seemed aware of him, falling asleep almost at once.

Then Daniel was free to settle down with the video-cassettes and papers. He wished he could remember more about what had happened. It wasn't uncommon for policemen to forget details in time, as other cases took over, but he'd always been known in the force for his phenomenal memory. Not with this case, though. His mind seemed to have wiped it out.

He tried an old trick. Stop worrying about the thing you needed to remember. Go back to something that had happened earlier and work forward. But that meant reviving a memory he flinched from; of how a gentle, loving woman and a bright-faced little boy had been mowed down in a car driven by Carter Denroy, a lout with booze running in his veins, a man so drunk that he couldn't afterward remember what had happened. And that led to another terrible memory— Denroy walking from court, a free man, smirking because his only punishment had been a fine. That smirk had burned itself into Daniel's consciousness so deeply that it still tortured his dreams.

He wanted to shy away now, but he forced himself to relive the scene, and gradually another detail emerged. There had been a woman there, too. A glossy, expensive woman who'd looked bored and impatient with the whole business of coming to court, as though it was simply too ridiculous to make a man pay for the lives he destroyed. As Denroy and the woman had walked out together, Daniel had heard her say, "You see, I told you it would be all right."

Daniel had stepped out quietly to stand in front of them, which had made the grin fade from Denroy's face. He'd halted, saying nothing, looking nervous. But the woman hadn't been nervous. She'd looked Daniel up and down before saying imperiously, "Kindly get out of our way."

Daniel had neither moved nor spoken. He'd just stood looking at the man who'd killed his wife, his face possessed by a cold, silent hate that had made Denroy flinch. He'd been scared. Was that what had made him say such a stupid, fatuous thing? *No hard feelings, eh?*

Just an accident. Then he'd fallen back at the menace in Daniel's face.

Now Daniel remembered how Denroy had cast a nervous glance at the woman, and how her contempt had seemed to force some courage into him—enough courage to shoulder his way past. That look had told Daniel all he'd needed to know about their relationship. Denroy had been intimidated by her, had wanted to impress her. That was why he'd driven her home when he'd had no right to be behind the wheel of a car. He'd probably bragged, "Don't worry. What's a little booze? I can handle it."

Daniel had thought of Denroy often, but the woman had faded from his mind—until now.

Another memory—Canvey, there with him in court, hovering beside him as he'd confronted his wife's killers, hands at the ready to stop him from physically attacking Denroy. He was a good friend. He'd hauled Daniel away to the nearest pub and poured drink down him. "Take some time off," he'd said. "Take as much as you need."

"I can cope," he'd insisted.

"You think you can, but you shouldn't work in this state."

"I tell you, I can cope."

He'd prided himself on being a hard man, a strong man who could stand up to anything. He'd thrown himself into his job, working all hours, ignoring weariness, driving himself to the limit. It was the only way he could endure. Canvey had been concerned. "I see you staring into space sometimes," he'd said, "and when I say your name, you don't seem to hear."

Daniel had responded by driving himself even harder. Whether he'd done his work well or not was something he didn't know, because he could hardly recall a single detail of that time.

But he *had* to remember. He forced his mind back. Henry Grainger. Hang on to that name. Henry Grainger, the owner of a small block of apartments, had been found dead. Someone had hit him over the head with a blunt instrument. Daniel had been sent to investigate.

All the signs pointed to Mrs. Megan Anderson, one of Grainger's tenants, who'd been heard quarreling with him the night he'd died. He hadn't been found until the following evening, at which time Mrs. Anderson was out on an assignment for an escort agency. Daniel had waited until she'd returned late that night. She'd walked in, glossy, expensive, consciously alluring, dressed and made up for effect. He recalled that she'd made that impression on him, but strangely, he couldn't conjure up her face. Instead he kept seeing the face of Denroy's companion, who'd also been glossy and heavily made up. He tried hard to concentrate, but he couldn't clear the confusion, and at last he gave up and put a cassette into the video machine.

For a moment he didn't even recognize the woman who appeared on the screen. Surely she couldn't be the same person as the tense, feverish invalid upstairs? The contrast shocked him. He stared at the screen, noting her defiance, almost arrogance, tinged with bafflement at finding herself in a police station under suspicion of murder.

He heard his own off-camera voice. "Let's go back to your quarrel with Mr. Grainger, Mrs. Anderson."

"It wasn't a quarrel," the woman on the screen said wearily. "I didn't know him well enough to quarrel with. He tried to paw me about, I told him to push off."

"That's not what your neighbors say. According to them, the whole thing was very violent."

"They weren't there. I was."

"They heard screaming and shouting."

"I was angry. He disgusted me. He was a worm."

"That's how you saw him, was it? A worm?"

Such an obvious trap, he thought now, but she hadn't seen it. "Yes, a worm," she said with a shrug. "Or a sewer rat. Take your pick."

Wouldn't a woman have to be innocent to walk so blindly into danger? he wondered. He almost winced as he heard his own voice springing the trap. "In other words, vermin—to be destroyed? A worm to be trodden on. A rat to be hit on the head—like Henry Grainger?"

"I didn't kill him. He was alive when I left the building. I walked miles away. I told you that before."

"Yes, you told me you went to Wimbledon Common. I've got a team out there trying to find someone who saw you. But so far there are no witnesses to confirm that you were there."

The words brought Daniel out in a cold sweat. There *had* been a witness. He'd been lying, unless . . .

He leafed frantically through the papers until he came to the photocopied statement from the man who'd seen "a woman who might have been Megan Anderson," on Wimbledon Common at the time Grainger had been killed. There was a note scribbled on it in Daniel's own writing, saying he'd received it on February twenty-third. He yanked the cassette from the machine to study the label, but in his haste to duplicate everything, he hadn't made notes. But it would be on the cassette, at the very start. His heart thumping madly, he shoved the cassette in, rewound it and pressed the play button. In the few seconds it took the machine to start, he felt as if he was dying.

Then his own voice, "Mrs. Megan Anderson being questioned by Detective Inspector Keller in Interview Room 10. Interview timed at fifteen hundred hours, February twenty-first. Let's go back to..."

The twenty-first. Two days before the statement. He hadn't been lying to trap her. The relief was so overwhelming that he almost blacked out. When he'd steadied himself, he poured a stiff drink and wondered at the pass he'd come to. It was appalling to have to rely on outside evidence to confirm his honesty to himself, but he had no recollection of either the statement or the interview.

He ran the tape forward to where he'd left off. "...no witnesses to confirm that you were there. It's a pity you can't remember seeing anyone else there."

"I wasn't looking at other people," Megan said. "I just walked there to be alone and brood on how much Henry Grainger disgusted me."

Her tone struck him. She sounded bored, exasperated and edgy, but not frightened, as though she knew this was only a misunderstanding that was bound to be cleared up in the end. It was a tone he associated with innocence, and he wondered if he'd noticed it at the time.

This interview had taken place two days after Grainger's death. She'd changed from the gorgeous evening wear of their first meeting, but she was still smartly dressed and groomed. A lot of care had been applied to her face, as though beauty was a tool of her trade.

He saw himself appear on the screen. Evidently he'd risen and walked around the table to confront her more closely: he sat on the table in front of her and leaned down. Watching himself, he made a face of distaste at what looked like an intimidatory tactic. But the woman he confronted wasn't intimidated. She raised her head and looked up at him coolly, defiantly. He felt a flicker of admiration now for the way she wouldn't back down in front of a bully.

A bully? Himself? Yes. The sound of his own voice grated on him. "Tell me about it from the beginning, Mrs. Anderson."

"Oh, God, not again! I've told you so often."

Suddenly his face came into view, and he was shocked. He looked like a dead man, a zombie, and it was a dead man's voice that said, "Tell me again. Let's see if you can remember any details you've forgotten."

Daniel shivered.

Three

After three days of feeling too ill to care about anything, Megan awoke to the discovery that the fever had left her and her body no longer ached. Getting gingerly out of bed, she found that she was still weak, but after being unable to eat anything she was now ravenously hungry. She put on the thick socks Daniel always left for her feet, pulled on his robe, and left the room, holding on to things as she moved. The house was a big, rambling building that looked as if it might have been built a century ago. Although clean, it was shabby and in need of redecorating. Glancing out the window, she saw a large garden with trees and a rockery, the sort of garden that cried out for dogs and children romping together. But it was empty.

Everywhere was silence and there was no sign of Daniel. What Megan could see of the house was austere, as though its occupant lived in it only in passing.

One room was different. It was at the back of the house, and it was filled with electronic gadgets, audio-video equipment, tapes, records, magazines. How like Daniel Keller, she thought, to have a hobby that offered him the world at a distance. It fitted her picture of him as a man without human feeling.

She glanced idly through the videocassettes strewn on the floor. Their labels bore hastily scrawled notes in pencil. One of them read Interview 3. Feb. 23rd, 19—

Her heart began to beat hard. February 23rd was the day of her third interview with Keller. But surely...?

She hurried, switched on the set, and shoved the cassette into the machine. Shocked, she saw her own angry face on the screen. And from off camera came Daniel's voice, taunting her. "You could have killed him easily. He wasn't a big man, and I'll bet you're not as fragile as you look."

Then the woman on the screen did the worst possible thing. Losing her temper, she launched herself forward at her tormentor. For a moment Daniel came into the shot, fending her off. He was right. She *was* stronger than she looked, and he had some trouble keeping her nails from his face. "Was this how you went for Henry Grainger with that heavy ashtray?" he asked, gasping slightly.

"I didn't kill him."

"The ashtray had your fingerprints and nobody else's except Grainger's own. How do you account for that?"

Megan shut off the set, shaking. She tried to calm her own thoughts. If she brooded about how much she hated Keller, it would overset her mind, and she needed her wits about her. Quickly she pulled out the cassette and began to rummage through the others, which all turned out to be copies of her interviews in the police station. The last thing she came to was a thick, buff-colored envelope, which she accidentally knocked off the sofa, sending its contents spilling over the floor. Gathering them up, she found herself looking at her own face.

Amazed, she studied the other papers. Every one of them was a piece about herself from her modeling days. Most were straightforward fashion shots, in which she was wearing a succession of glamorous clothes. One was a magazine cover, showing a close-up of her face, looking sensual and gorgeous. Megan considered the beauty in that picture as if she were a stranger, which in a sense was true. She had nothing to do with the shattered woman regarding her now.

There were some pages attached to the cover, containing a feature about her from inside the magazine. It was headlined, Tiger Lady and the writer had started by quoting Blake's "Tyger, tyger, burning bright/In the forests of the night." From there he'd gone wild, lavishing purple prose over "a woman with the power and sultry eroticism of a tiger, who moves with the sleek, silent grace of a jungle creature, stalking the forests of the night."

The first time Megan had read it she'd laughed, thinking it wildly overdone. Now she wondered who that proud, confident woman had been, and how she'd ever come to this pass.

What astonished her most was finding the piece here, along with the copies of her interviews with Keller. It looked as though he'd been studying her in some depth. But why? Was he seeking the truth after all this time, or merely trying to confirm his original verdict? She decided it was probably safest to think badly of him. He was concerned with saving his own face and rebuilding his life. The rebuilding of *her* life wouldn't concern him.

Megan rose suddenly and began to search for the telephone, which she found in an alcove in the hall. It was nearly four o'clock. Tommy would have just arrived home from school. If she called now there was a chance that he might pick up the phone. With trembling hands she dialed the number and sat, white-knuckled, listening to the ringing on the other end. So intent was she that she didn't hear the front door open and Daniel come quietly into the house.

At last there was an answer. Megan's heart sank as she heard the voice of Brian's mother. "I want to speak to Tommy," she said as firmly as she could.

"I've told you before, that isn't possible," said Mrs. Anderson in the cool, inflexible voice that Megan hated. "Please don't call again."

"I'll call as often as I have to," she raged. "He's my son, and you can't keep him from me."

"Whatever his father and I do is in the child's best interests. Kindly try to understand that, and don't keep pestering us." The phone went dead.

Megan had always disliked her self-righteous mother-in-law, but in the past she'd had the emotional stamina to cope with her. Now, with her nerves in shreds, she had no stamina left. She slammed down the receiver and thumped her fists helplessly against the wall again and again.

"Hey, come on." Daniel reached out and touched her shoulder. Megan swung away, staring at him. "That doesn't help," he said gently.

"Nothing helps," she said frantically. "But it relieves my feelings, until the next time."

"Was that your husband you were talking to?"

"His mother. She won't let me talk to Tommy."

"Let's have a cup of tea," he suggested, leading the way to the kitchen. She followed him and watched while he put the kettle on. "It's good to see you up and looking better," he said.

"I don't remember much about what happened. I ran away into the park . . . didn't I?"

"That's right. I followed you there and brought you here. You were soaked. I haven't tried to get your things back from the boarding house in case the press is still sniffing around and it leads them here."

"There was nothing I cared about," she said with a shrug. "Just the things they give prisoners when they're discharged." She looked down at his robe and nightwear. "What happened to my nightgown?"

"I sent it to the laundry. It isn't back yet."

"There was no need to take that trouble," she said, glancing at the washing machine. "Just throw it in."

He was embarrassed. Having stripped the soaking nightgown off her without a second thought, he'd discovered that an unsuspected sense of propriety had made him avoid washing it himself, even in a machine. But he flinched from explaining this, anticipating her derision. "I was afraid you'd be really ill," he said, concentrating on the kettle, "so I called in my doctor—a woman doctor. She looked after you. Here, the tea's ready."

She accepted the mug and sipped it. "I don't like depending on you," she said. "I'll call my lawyer, and she'll help me."

They looked at each other warily. "I'd rather help you myself," Daniel said.

"Look, I'm grateful to you for nursing me, but basically nothing's changed. I just want to move out."

"But not today. I need to talk to you first. We have . . . a lot to talk about."

She regarded him ironically. "Didn't we talk enough three years ago?"

"We talked a lot, but maybe not to any good purpose. I've been through those interviews, and there are things I'm uneasy about."

"You're . . . ?" She regarded him in cynical hilarity. "You're uneasy. Now I've heard everything. There were one or two things I was uneasy about, too, in particular, the way you deliberately distorted the truth and wrecked my life. Don't ever imagine that pouring a few aspirin down my throat makes up for it."

"I wouldn't expect it to, if I really had deliberately hidden the truth," he said edgily. His anger was rising as he discovered how difficult it was to make any impression on her. He was used to being arrogant, dominant, as a policeman had to be. Eating humble pie came very hard to him. "But I didn't."

"Oh, come on," she said wearily. "We've passed that point, surely?"

"Megan, I didn't suppress that statement," he said emphatically. "I simply didn't remember it."

She raised an eyebrow at him. "You can do better than that."

"No, I can't, because it's true. I didn't remember anything about the witness. My mind just . . . blanked him out." In despair he could hear how unconvincing it sounded, and her look of derision confirmed it. Perhaps if he told her everything about his mental and emotional agony at that time, and what had caused it, she might understand. But something deep within him

shied away from exposing his wounds. He'd never
begged for mercy. It wasn't his way. "I had . . . a lot of
cases on my plate" was the best he could manage.

"Funny, that. You always seemed to have time to
interrogate me," she observed. "I've never heard such
a feeble excuse. What are you? Some kind of incom-
petent who needs your hand held? At least suppress-
ing evidence is decisive. Losing it because you're
muddled is the action of a wimp."

His temper rose. "You make very glib judgments,"
he snapped.

"So did you."

"The evidence against you was very strong. Without that witness it was a rock-solid case."

"And of course you made absolutely sure it was
'without that witness.'"

"Will you listen to me?" he demanded hoarsely.

"Will listening to you make any difference?" she
flung back at him. "Will it give me back my reputation, three years of my life—*my son?* How would you
know what it's like to lose your child and think about
him every moment of every day, becoming obsessed
with him because they had no right to take him but he's
gone anyway?" She took a deep, shuddering breath
and forced herself to calm down. "There's no point in
going through it again. You know what you did, even
if you won't admit it. There must be a way to undo the
damage you did. I just . . . just don't know what it is."

He could have given her the answer. There was only
one way to clear her completely, and that was to find
the real murderer. But he didn't say so because he still
wasn't totally convinced. After the days spent studying the interviews, he had serious doubts, but that

wasn't enough. He caught her looking at him, and had an uncomfortable feeling that she'd read his thoughts.

"I'm going to call my lawyer," she said. "The sooner I'm away from here, the better." She went back to the alcove and dialed.

"Newton and Baines," the receptionist at the other end said.

"I'd like to speak to Janice," Megan said urgently.

"I'm afraid Mrs. Baines isn't here. Her son has measles and she's quarantined at home with him."

Megan ground her nails into her palm. "Mr. Newton, then."

"One moment."

She was reluctant to talk to Newton, a curt man who seemed devoid of all human sympathy, but she was desperate. When he came on the line a moment later her worst fears were realized. He listened in frozen silence as she described her predicament, then said, "I must say I think you were extremely unwise to leave your lodging."

"I was driven out. I can't go back there."

"But you appear to have found somewhere else, so I don't see the problem."

Megan tried to keep her temper. "I am *temporarily* in the home of Detective Inspector Keller, the man who put me away, and *that* is the problem."

"I don't understand. What are you doing there?"

"He rescued me from the press and brought me here. But I've been here nearly a week, and I don't want to stay."

"Hmm." Newton sounded bored. "Well, frankly, Mrs. Anderson, I find your point of view hard to comprehend. Having managed to get this man on your side, your sensible course would surely be to make use of him. He has, er, resources denied the rest of us. Give me the address and I'll arrange for some money to be sent to you, but I'm afraid it won't be much."

As she hung up, Daniel came out into the hall and looked at her inquiringly. "She's away," Megan said. "Her partner is going to send me some money."

"If you need money, why did you run away from the press?" he asked wryly. "They were offering to buy your story. You could have told the world just what you thought of me. I can't think why you passed up the chance."

"Because my son might have seen it. I don't want him picking up a newspaper and seeing Megan Anderson Tells All. Brian would claim it made me an unfit mother, and I have enough of a fight on my hands without giving him ammunition."

"Won't he give you some financial help?"

"*Him?*" Megan asked with withering scorn. "All he wants is for me to vanish from sight. It suited him to have me in prison where I couldn't challenge him for Tommy. Now that I'm out, he'd like to pretend it hasn't happened."

She sipped her tea in brooding silence, not noticing what he was doing until he placed a plate of bacon and eggs in front of her. "Eat up," he said. "You haven't had a proper meal for days, and it takes strength to hate someone as much as you hate me."

She thought she couldn't touch anything he'd cooked, but after the first mouthful she couldn't stop herself. It was delicious. When she could spare the time to speak, she said, "I've lived on hate. I'd almost forgotten what anything else tastes like. You're a good cook. I'll admit that. I suppose I really should thank you for taking care of me."

Daniel managed a faint grin that briefly lightened the habitual sternness of his face. "Don't force yourself if it's hard. Having led the press to you, I had to rescue you."

"I suppose your appearance on the scene gave them an even better story."

He shook his head. "I've been watching the papers. One or two of them said you'd been found and escaped. One of them mentioned a 'mystery man,' but nobody realized it was me. We were lucky. The light was poor, and they didn't recognize me."

"Well, I'll swear that's the first piece of luck I've ever had where you're concerned."

"What I said still holds. I'm the best guarantee of your anonymity while we sort things out."

"Sort things out? What do you have in mind?"

"You're in a kind of limbo. We can't just leave things there."

"Is that why you've been going through the evidence?"

"How did you know that?"

"I've seen the room where you keep the tapes."

"Did you look at them?"

"Only briefly. I remember it all pretty well without help. What is this, Mr. Keller? An attack of conscience?"

"Don't you think you could call me Daniel? Or is that too much to ask?"

"Much too much," she told him.

"All right. I've been going through those tapes, trying to remember the details...to work out where I went wrong—"

"Will it make any difference?"

"I'm not sure, but I have to try. If you're innocent—" He stopped, realizing that anything he could
say would be dangerous.

Megan was looking at him wryly. "Yes," she said.
"My innocence really causes you problems, doesn't
it?"

"So would your guilt," he growled. "Okay, let's
leave it for the moment."

For the first few weeks in prison, Megan's sleep had
been haunted by nightmares. They'd returned when she
was released, but for the past few nights, although her
dreams had been feverish and disjointed, they hadn't
been painful. But this night she was gripped again by
anguish. Tommy was just out of sight, but when she
tried to reach him, Brian stood there, blocking her
path. She tried to get past him but he fought her off.
She lashed out blindly, screaming at him to let her go,
but he was too strong for her.

Suddenly his face changed and became the face of
Daniel Keller. She fought harder. He didn't fight back,
but held her, saying, "Hey, come on, it's all right, wake
up. *Wake up, Megan.*"

She finally managed to awaken, to find that she was
in bed and Daniel really was there, holding her. "Wake
up," he said again.

She was gasping as if she'd been running hard. "It
was a bad dream," she said. "I'm all right."

"Are you sure? You were screaming."

"I was trying to find Tommy. That's all there is in
the world now, trying to find Tommy. Brian was keeping me away, and when I tried to get past him, he
turned into you."

He grimaced. "The villain always turns into me, doesn't he?"

She sighed. "You know the answer to that." He was still holding her and she turned her body to edge away from him. His pajama jacket was much too large for her and the slight movement made it slide halfway down her arms, exposing her breasts. She drew in her breath and snatched at the jacket, pulling the edges together at her throat.

Daniel snatched his hands away and rose from the bed, moving backward quickly, staring at her in dismay. Somehow he made an excuse and got out, almost running to his own room. There he shut the door firmly and sat down on the bed, trying to stop himself from shaking. He stayed that way for a while, then went downstairs, hoping that a snack might restore his sense of proportion. But that didn't work, either.

He was thunderstruck, shattered by the unexpectedness of the moment and what it had done to him. It had been so fast, leaving him no time to steel himself against it.

Until now it had never occurred to him to see Megan as a sexual being. He'd loved his wife deeply, and her brutal death had numbed him to all normal instincts and sensations, so that for the past three years he hadn't desired any woman. He'd vaguely assumed that this would continue.

In one blinding instant everything had changed, not because he'd seen Megan's naked breasts, but because she'd hastened to cover them. That instinctive movement had betrayed an awareness of herself as a woman in the presence of a man, and by rejecting the possibility of sexuality between them, she had, paradoxically, made him conscious of it.

Memories and impressions crowded in on him: the sight of her in the park, her thin, sodden nightgown clinging to her; the feel of her near naked body in his arms as he'd carried her to the car; the sight of her pale, smooth flesh as he'd stripped off the nightgown and dried her. All these things had seemed to pass him by, leaving him free to act impersonally. But in fact they'd been lying in wait until the moment he was ready to recognize them. Now that moment had arrived, and suddenly there they were, running on feet as soft and silent as a tiger's, to spring at him out of the darkness. His senses were pervaded by her, possessed by her. His flesh seemed to sing with the memory of her. Every encounter had imprinted itself on his subconscious, waiting to be played back later with such vividness that it was like living them all over again.

He could almost have laughed out loud at the irony. It was a disaster, a hilarious disaster: a black, bitter joke against him. Was there a woman in the world who hated him more? Did he have a more relentless enemy? How crazy for him to become so blazingly aware of her! How ridiculous for his loins to ache for her, his heart to beat faster at the thought of her beauty. Ridiculous. Illogical. Outrageous. Absurd. Catastrophic. Something that shouldn't happen, that *couldn't* happen.

But it had happened.

For the rest of the night Megan lay very still in the darkness, listening to Daniel moving about the house. She heard him return to his bedroom and leave again after only a few minutes. There was the sound of his footsteps going downstairs, followed by the faint clatter of china in the kitchen. Then he went into the back room, and Megan heard the video-player being switched on. She could even make out the sound of her own voice, faint but perceptible.

She found it was easy to follow what was happening to him, what he was thinking. She'd been desired by too many men not to recognize the signs. The revelation that he wanted her had been like a flash of lightning, illuminating the landscape for one fierce, blazing second, showing her undreamed-of possibilities.

Newton's words came back to her. *Having managed to get this man on your side, your sensible course would surely be to make use of him.*

She'd dismissed the suggestion, but that was before she discovered that she had power over Daniel Keller. It had been there in his eyes, shocking him as much as it had shocked her. She'd seen that, too. Right this minute he was trying to fight it. His restless movements told her that. But he wouldn't succeed, because she would make sure he didn't.

She had a strange sensation of seeing everything in her life in clear, hard outline. What she was planning would once have been anathema to her, but prison had taught her endurance and survival. She'd always been a strong woman, but now she was strong enough to do anything she had to.

"That's enough," she whispered to herself. "You've been behaving like a victim, and now it's got to stop. It's *going* to stop. That man is your lifeline, and you're going to use him. He ruined your life, now he can put it right."

She sat up in bed. She was no longer talking out loud, but the words had mounted to a roar inside her head.

He deprived me of my reputation and my son. Now he's going to get them back for me and I don't care what I have to do to make him.

Four

Mr. Newton's check for two hundred pounds arrived the next morning. With it was a letter regretting that the amount could not be more, but the firm had only limited funds for such purposes, and while her compensation was still being negotiated...et cetera, et cetera.

Megan stared at the check indignantly. She'd hoped for a reasonable amount to give her a little independence. "He's not much help, is he?" Daniel asked, reading over her shoulder.

"None at all," she answered. "I dare say I can get some social assistance payments—"

"And be stared at," he reminded her. "Then the press will get to hear of it, and it'll all start again."

"I'll have to chance it. There's nothing else I can do."

Daniel knew he was standing on the verge of a precipice. He must get her out of here quickly. Every moment she was here she was a danger to him. The words he ought to speak whirled in his brain. *I'll lend you some money—enough to get you somewhere to live—away from here.* Say it *now*. Make it irrevocable while you still can.

At last he spoke. "You're welcome to stay here, but I suppose you'll throw that offer back in my teeth."

Megan hesitated for one split second on the edge of the resolution she'd made in the darkness the night before. Then the die was cast. "I might not," she said casually, and took an angry pleasure in seeing that he was taken aback yet reluctantly glad. He looked as if he hadn't slept all night.

"Then you'll stay?" he asked.

She shrugged. "I may as well. I'll need some clothes. Can you cash this check for me?"

"No problem."

As she had nothing to wear to go shopping, Daniel went upstairs and returned with a few basic things, including a dress and a coat. "These used to belong to my wife," he said briefly. "They're all I have of hers. You'll find them a little out of fashion, but serviceable."

"Don't worry," she told him, "I haven't been keeping up with fashion."

Half of her mind noted that they were in the style that had been popular when she'd gone to prison, but she was too preoccupied to read any significance into this. Daniel's wife had been sturdier in build than herself, and not as tall, but with the help of a needle and thread she managed to produce a passable result.

Daniel drove her into town, well away from the area where he was known.

Despite everything, Megan's spirits rose at being out and about after three years of gray walls. She received a nasty shock when she saw the prices, and realized that two hundred pounds would stretch even less than she'd thought. She resolved the problem by diving into a shop that Daniel would have overlooked. "It's only secondhand stuff in here," he objected.

"There can be treasures in secondhand shops if you know how to look," she told him.

She chose slacks and sweaters and a couple of dresses that could easily be altered. The only things she bought new were underwear and shoes. When she'd finished, she had thirty pounds left. "Enough for another pair of shoes," Daniel suggested.

"No, I have something else in mind. Will you wait for me here?"

She slipped away and found a shop selling makeup and perfume. She didn't want Daniel to know the details of what she bought there, but she was providing herself with vital weapons in her campaign to turn him into her instrument.

At home she offered him his wife's dress and coat back, but he refused with a brief shake of the head and a curt gesture that told her the subject was closed.

Gathering her purchases, Megan went up to her own room to work at altering the secondhand clothes. She was a skilled needlewoman, having picked up the hobby in prison, and when she'd finished, she had a reasonable wardrobe, one in which she looked good.

When she was ready, she dressed and applied makeup, but only very discreetly. Daniel was no fool and would be instantly suspicious of an obvious come-on. So when she went downstairs in the late afternoon she was conservatively dressed in a plain skirt and simple, unrevealing top, with makeup so subtly laid on that it might almost have been natural.

The door to the video room was closed, but she could hear sounds coming from behind it. The words were muffled, but it was her own voice, followed by Daniel's, then clicks, as if someone had stopped the tape to wind it back. He played the same section three times over before he was satisfied. Megan went quietly away into the kitchen.

Half an hour later she knocked on the door and called, "I've made something to eat."

He grunted his thanks for the food she set in front of him, and ate in abstracted silence. Megan left him to his thoughts until the meal was over, then said, "Did you find those tapes illuminating?"

"Not very. I've been over them so often now they're not making any impact anymore." He looked at her abruptly, as if he'd made a sudden resolution. "Megan, listen to me. There may be a way I can help you, but only if we go about it properly."

"What do you mean?"

"I want you to let me interview you again...like I did before."

"Oh, no," she said at once. "You've got all you want on those tapes."

"That's just what I haven't got. The interviews I did then are bad, clumsy. I missed so much. I want to do it differently...the way I should have done then." When he saw her torn by indecision, he demanded urgently, "What have you got to lose?"

She shrugged. "You're right. What do you want me to do?"

"Come with me." He led her into the living room and pointed to the sofa, while he took an armchair. "Sit and face me. Imagine it's three years ago. We're talking for the first time. Do you remember that?"

"Yes. I'd been out on a date for an escort agency. I came home to the apartment block and found the police there. Henry Grainger, the landlord, had been found dead that evening. He'd been killed the night before, but it was some hours before he was discovered. I went up to my apartment, and after a while there was a knock on the door. When I opened it, you were outside."

In his mind he saw the door being opened by the supremely beautiful, confident woman. She'd been wearing a red figure-hugging dress, and her glorious brown hair had spilled over her bare shoulders. In his mind he reproduced the face, its smoky sensuality skillfully accentuated by the careful makeup, and he recalled how the mere sight of that casually flaunted beauty had made his hackles rise. *But why?*

He took up the thread. "I told you Grainger had been found dead, and asked you about a quarrel you'd had with him the night before. Tell me about that quarrel now . . . as if it were then."

"He came to see me to remind me that I was behind with the rent. I told him I'd be able to pay in a couple of days, and he said, why didn't I pay him 'in kind.' That was how he put it."

"Did you ask him exactly what he meant by that?"

"There was no need. He'd made the suggestion before. He was always smarming around me, trying to touch me, making suggestive remarks. He was a horrid little man. He disgusted me, but I couldn't get rid of him."

"Why didn't you move to another address?"

"I wanted to, but I couldn't find a decent place at a rent I could afford. I found out that he was charging me a lower rent than the others in the block, to induce me to stay. I had no choice. He kept hinting that I ought to be 'nice' to him to make up the extra. I didn't do it, but I felt trapped."

"What about your husband—alimony—that sort of thing?"

"My husband was furious with me for taking our son. He was trying to starve me back to him."

"Where was your son that evening?"

"He was spending the night with the family of one of his school friends. He stayed the next night, too, because I was going to be out."

"Doing 'escort' work?"

"Yes, and let me make it plain that my escort work was just that—escort, and nothing else. I didn't do 'private' work on the side."

"Was there nothing else you could do?"

"Like what? I left school as soon as I could. I was a model at sixteen. Jobs are hard to come by even for people with qualifications. I did a little modeling—"

"Do," he interrupted.

"What was that?"

"You *do* a little modeling. This is three years ago. We've been allowing ourselves to forget that, and we shouldn't. It's important."

"You can't turn the clock back like that," she protested.

"It's the only way we can make this work. You and I have just met for the first time. We never saw each other before. There are no . . . ghosts . . . between us."

"No ghosts, or no guilt?" she challenged him. "Can you wipe your guilt out by pretending it doesn't exist?"

He gritted his teeth. "We have to pretend that *everything* doesn't exist."

She sat regarding him for a moment. "All right," she said at last. "In that case, I have some changes to make." She hurried from the room and went upstairs. She was gone half an hour. It was longer than she'd intended, but she wanted to get everything just right. What would have been wrong earlier in the evening was right now. When she was satisfied, she smiled at herself in the mirror. She'd made her decision. Now it was time to carry it through.

She had her reward when she returned to him and saw the shock in his eyes as he took in the change in her. Gone were the demure skirt and top, replaced by a pair of figure-hugging slacks. The knitted top buttoned down the front and had a low neck that just revealed the swelling of her breasts. The glamour had been laid onto her face like a mask. "That wasn't necessary," he said roughly.

"Oh, but it was. You're trying to reproduce that first interview as closely as possible, but it wasn't pale, dreary Megan Anderson you interviewed. It was Tiger Lady, and you hated her. Come on, Daniel, admit it. You hated everything about her, hated her so much that—"

"That's enough," he broke in harshly.

"No, it isn't. You're the one who wanted to relive the past, so let's relive that bit—the bit where you hated me at first sight."

He hated her now for the wounds she was reopening and the turmoil she was creating inside him. He couldn't tell her that reliving the past had become suddenly difficult. Back in those days he'd looked on her exotic beauty with indifference, his heart buried, his senses dead. Now his senses had flamed back to life. She was forbidden fruit: forbidden by every law of common sense and sheer self-preservation. But last night the desire to touch her had come blazing out of nowhere to inflame and engulf him. And the more he fought it, the more it possessed him.

"All right," he said at last, with an effortful assumption of indifference. "Let's do it this way. You were saying that you do a little modeling."

She moved languidly across the room and dropped into the sofa opposite him, leaning back and looking at him. Everything about her was graceful. "I don't earn much by modeling," she said. "I'm over twenty-five, way past my best."

He studied his notes, refusing to look at her. "Tell me about what happened between you and Grainger that evening."

"Nothing happened. That was the point. Nothing was ever going to happen, but he couldn't get that into his head. I said no in a dozen different ways, but he wouldn't accept it. Then he started trying to paw me."

"And you reacted violently, according to your neighbors."

"I yelled at him, yes. I called him all the names I could think of. Why not?"

"You did a bit more than call him names, didn't you?"

"I told you, he tried to paw me. There was a struggle. I threw him out."

"And called something after him as he went downstairs?"

"I told him he wasn't fit to live. I should think the whole building must have heard me. But I didn't kill him."

"What did you do when he'd gone?"

"I dashed out. I wanted to get as far away from the building as possible. I walked and walked for hours. I couldn't—can't—afford a car. I ended up on Wimbledon Common, *where someone saw me.*"

"Where someone saw a woman who answered your general description," Daniel reminded her.

"At exactly the time I said I was there."

"It helps, but it's not conclusive."

"I was there. Your forensic experts said Grainger died at three o'clock in the morning. I left the building at midnight and I didn't get back until seven."

"Unless you'd taken a taxi."

"So now you've got a taxi driver who dropped me at the block in time for me to kill Grainger?"

"No, but I've only your word for it that you ever left the building."

"Plus the witness on Wimbledon Common," she insisted.

"All right. Plus the witness on Wimbledon Common. What happened when you got back?"

"The room was still a mess from our struggle. I tidied it up and wiped the corner of the mantelpiece. He'd fallen against it when we struggled, and it split his lip."

"You didn't tell me that the first time," Daniel said, stopping her quickly.

"Yes, I did."

"Not at the first meeting. You didn't mention it until two days later, after I'd had forensic tests done on the clothes you were wearing that night, and found Grainger's blood."

"Thus proving that I invented the story of the struggle to account for his blood?"

"Proving nothing. I just wished you'd mentioned it earlier."

"I was confused and upset. Haven't you ever been in such a state that you couldn't think straight? No, of course not. You wouldn't begin to know what it's like."

"I might," he said after a moment.

"Not you."

"You criticized me for making glib judgments, Megan. Be careful you don't make them yourself."

"I've had a lot of time to make my judgments about you. Three years."

"But you didn't know all the facts," he said quickly.

"So tell me the facts. Let's talk about you, Daniel."

There it was again, the chance to make her understand how ill and distraught he'd been three years ago, and perhaps remove that cold, judgmental look from her eyes, perhaps even soften her so that she would let him reach out and—

"This isn't doing any good," he said harshly. "We should try to keep to the point. Grainger's blood was found in your apartment."

"But his body was found downstairs," she reminded him. When he hesitated, she gave a little smile and said, "Then you have to say, 'You could have killed him easily. He wasn't a big man, and I'll bet you're not as fragile as you look.'"

"Did I say that?" Daniel asked awkwardly.

"Oh, come on, we're being honest. I've looked at those tapes, which means *you* certainly have. How come they let you remove them from the station?"

"They didn't. I got copies."

"Why?" she asked quickly.

Realizing what he'd given away, he shrugged and prevaricated. "Does it matter?"

She shook her head, smiling, and he knew he'd revealed too much about the inner turmoil she was causing him. Although they were reenacting the interrogation, he had the uneasy feeling that she'd somehow taken command. "Let's get back to the point," he said uneasily.

"All right. You said I wasn't as fragile as I looked, and I did the stupidest thing, didn't I? I proved you right by losing my temper and flying at you like this—"

She launched herself at him suddenly. He rose and put up his arms, trying to fend her off without actually taking hold of her, but she renewed the attack until in the end he was forced to seize her. For a few moments they struggled until he managed to imprison her in his arms, holding her tightly. She looked up at him, her face flushed from the struggle, her eyes alight with an emotion he didn't understand, but which was actually triumph. She'd drawn him further into her spell. She knew it from the thunder of his heart that she could feel against her own, from the rasping sound of his breathing, and from the look on his face as he stared down at her: part unease, part desire, part alarm.

The pounding of his heart had communicated itself to her own, so that it, too, was beating madly. A hot sweetness streamed through her body, and she knew it was the sweetness of revenge. To turn the tables on the man whose prey she'd been and make him *her* prey, to know that he was becoming as helpless in her clutches as she had been in his—that was pleasure. "I forget how the next bit went," she breathed. "What did we do?"

He loosened his grip on her and placed his hands on either side of her head, twining his fingers in her hair. His chest was rising and falling rapidly, and she could feel the force of his struggle in her own flesh. "We—"

"Yes . . . tell me—"

A shudder convulsed him. With an effort he freed himself from her. "I pushed you away from me," he said hoarsely.

She was disappointed, but only a little. She'd always known she was contending with a strong man, a hard man, who wouldn't fall easily. It would make his eventual subjugation doubly satisfying. "And you asked me if this was how I'd gone for Henry Grainger," she reminded him.

Daniel took a deep breath and forcibly pulled himself together. He felt buffeted by a whirlwind. "Ashtray," he said. "He was killed with an ashtray. It had your fingerprints on it, and nobody else's."

"It was mine. I've never denied it. But I didn't take it down to his flat, *he* did. That was one of his charming little habits. He'd call on me on some feeble pretext or other, and when he left he'd steal something of mine so that I had to go to his place to get it back. When I got there he'd apologize, pretend to have lost it, offer me a drink, anything to drag it out. It was that kind of sneaky behavior that made me loathe him. Are you seriously suggesting that I took my own ashtray down to kill him, and then forgot to take it away?"

"That was always the weakest part of the case against you," he conceded. "But it was the murder weapon, and it had your prints on it."

"Since it belonged to me, that's hardly surprising."

"There was no doubt that it was used to kill him."

"But not by me. Look, I know you don't have to prove motive—you told me that often enough—but did it never worry you that I didn't *have* a motive?"

"You loathed him. You've admitted it."

"That's a motive for kicking his shins, not for killing him. Good grief, if I killed every man who's tried to paw me in my life I'd be knee-deep in corpses by now."

He wished she hadn't put on the glamorous mask. It took him back in time in a way he didn't want. He tried to fight down his antagonism, but he couldn't prevent it infusing his voice. "I believe you. There must have been quite a few men who wanted you."

She shook her head so that her glorious hair swirled about her shoulders, and stood with her arms folded, regarding him satirically. "Yes, there have. After all, look at my career—first modeling, then escort work. That practically makes me a scarlet woman, doesn't it?"

"No, but it makes you Tiger Lady."

"Don't tell me you were blinded by that stuff, too?" she demanded with an ironic humor that mocked his naiveté. "It was all a load of publicists' nonsense. Inside I'm just like any other woman."

He looked down at her flushed face and glowing brown eyes. "No," he said slowly, "you're not just like any other woman. You never could be."

"That's it, isn't it? Tiger Lady was different—guilty from the start."

"That's nonsense."

"No, it isn't. There was something about me that set your back up the moment you saw me."

"We're getting off the point," he said, wishing she'd stop this.

"But it's true, isn't it? What was it that made you hate me?"

"I don't know," he said somberly.

"Is it still there? Do you hate me now as you did then?" Helplessly, he shook his head. "What do you feel this minute?" she persisted. "Tell me."

Desperation made him candid. "I don't need to tell you. A woman who's been pursued by so many men must know it when she sees it."

A speculative smile touched her lips. This was proving easier than she'd thought. "Perhaps," she murmured.

"Does that please you, Megan?" he mocked. "Is that what you really want, to make me your slave like the others, so that you can enjoy kicking me in the teeth? Would that give you satisfaction?"

"I have no plans for kicking you in the teeth," she told him softly.

"So what's in your mind? You had a reason for changing your clothes, and it wasn't just authenticity. You were determined to make me say that I want you—"

"I don't need to hear you say it," she reminded him.

"That's right. I gave myself away last night, and that's when you decided...what? Just how far into the net do you want to lure me?"

"Why don't you try and find out?" she suggested.

The suggestion was too much for him. With a low growl from his very depths, he pulled her against him and smothered her mouth with his own. There was madness in the passion that swept over him, engulfing him in its pounding urgency. Everything about this situation was insane. He knew that, but he was helpless in the grasp of sensations that he'd never experienced before. Her lips parted under his, inviting his tongue into the dark, hot depths, where there was mystery and magic. He could feel her luring him on, deliberately offering herself up to his passion, provoking him with the touch of her hands and the caresses of her lips. A tiny part of his mind that was still able to think asked, *Why?* But the question was drowned in the roar of his senses.

He ran his hands over the soft, pliant body that was pressed against him. It was slender but curved, the body of an experienced woman, who instinctively understood sensual pleasure and knew how to tease it alive in a man. Had she teased Henry Grainger to destruction, and then stamped on him like a worm when he got out of control? Part of him said it was impossible. The woman in his arms was all sweet, feminine urgency. She was the way a woman should be, eager and responsive, inciting and surrendering at the same moment.

But there was also something else, an undertone that was dark and fierce and hinted at primitive regions of her soul. It was alarming, thrilling and enticing at the same time.

The questions tormented him. He had a million facts on file about her life, and yet he knew nothing about her. There were two opposing pictures—either a murderess, or a deeply wronged woman—and he had no idea which one was the truth.

"Did you do it?" he heard his own voice asking hoarsely. "Tell me." But even as he asked, he kissed her wildly on her eyes, her face, her mouth, her neck.

"Do you think I did?" she taunted him.

"I don't know."

She lay back in his arms and looked at him through half-closed lids. "Well that's a step in the right direction," she murmured in a voice that hovered on the edge of a laugh. "Once, you were very sure you knew."

"And now I'm not, is that it? Do you think confusing me is the answer?"

She smiled hazily. "And you are confused, aren't you, Daniel?"

"Yes, damn you, I am."

"Never mind. Kiss me, Daniel. You know you want to. And you want more than that, don't you?"

He hesitated, torn by a struggle that was harder than anything in his life before.

Megan looked up at him, observing every expression on his face. At exactly the right moment she sank onto the sofa, leaning back against the cushions and pulling him down toward her. He covered her mouth again, kissing her with fierce intensity.

Megan returned his kiss with equal force. Part of her was observing everything that happened, watching him being drawn further into Tiger Lady's net, but to her alarm, something unforeseen was happening to her. The anger and bitterness that should have kept her safe in Daniel's arms were melting under the onslaught of his passion. Ripples of excitement were beginning to scurry through her body, going faster and faster until they overtook each other and became one pulsating rhythm. She tried to ignore it and keep her mind on what she thought of as her mission, but there was simply no way to ignore the relentless pounding of her heart, or the tremors that were set off wherever he touched her.

Irrational anger rose in her breast. How *dare* he do this to her? How dare he thrill her and set her body aflame as no other man, including Brian, had ever been able to do? He was her enemy, yet his touch was like electricity, igniting sparks that started on her skin and glittered right through her. She fought them, striving not to be conscious of physical delight, to think only of subduing her enemy and bending him to her will. But her enemy had enchantment in his touch. It made her crave what was forbidden, like the caress of his fingers against her breast. When she felt him pulling open the buttons of her top, she arched up against him and threw her head back, inviting him to trail kisses down her neck to the base of her throat.

She put her hand behind his head, drawing it lower so that his mouth was against her breast. Lightning forked through her as his lips drifted across the sensitive skin, and a long moan broke from her. What was happening was so wrong. It wasn't in her plan—somehow she must cling to her plan—but the pleasure taking possession of her made a mockery of calculation.

She was alive to every movement of his body, the feel of his hand sliding lower, opening more buttons, cupping the fullness of one breast in his palm, the fingers and thumb moving to tease the nipple. She knew that at any moment he would start working on the fastening to her slacks, and soon they would both be naked, ready for each other. She was tense with thrilling expectation. Soon—

But the movement he made wasn't the one she'd expected, craved. She felt a convulsion possess his body, then he became totally still. Megan touched him and found that he'd turned to stone.

"No." The cry was torn from him.

"Daniel—"

"*No.* Not like this!" Daniel wrenched himself free and backed away from Megan as though her touch burned him. "Dear God, what am I doing?" he breathed. The desire in his eyes had been replaced by anger. "I nearly fell for it, didn't I?" he demanded.

"Fell...for w-what?" she stammered, trying to collect her wits.

"Don't act innocent. I don't know what you're playing at, but I do know that you've got your own agenda."

The letdown caused a violent revulsion of feeling inside Megan, making her horribly aware of her open buttons and exposed breasts. She hastened to cover herself, trying to calm her breathing.

Daniel was watching her through narrowed eyes. "You were making me jump through hoops, weren't you?"

"I don't know what you're talking about," she prevaricated. She knew this was a disaster.

"I'm talking about a woman who hates me in the morning and melts in my arms in the evening. No, not melts. Scorches is more like it. You sent me up in flames and you came on as if you were in flames yourself, but *why?* Is that how Tiger Lady gets her kicks?"

"Don't call me that," she cried desperately. "It's not *me.*"

"So I nearly thought, until you showed your claws. But they were a little too sharp. I'm a plain man, Megan. I don't play sophisticated games, and I don't like them. So what's going on?"

"Nothing," she said desperately. "It was a mistake. Forget it."

She tried to pass him but he took her arm and forced her to face him. "Was it for the pleasure of making a fool of me, or was there an even more devious plan? Was I to be something more than a fool...an instrument, maybe?" This came so close to the truth that she flushed. He saw it and his hand tightened. "So that's it. I have my uses, don't I? I'll bet you never even realized that you could use me until last night, but then Tiger Lady's brain started working. Get the poor sap in a lather for you and he'll do anything...like clearing your name. Very clever. Very cunning. Very calculated. And to think I was beginning to feel sorry for you."

"Let me go," she cried.

"I'll let you go all right. Tomorrow morning you are out of this house for good. Got that?"

Megan didn't answer. She wrenched herself out of his grasp and flew upstairs, away from his condemning eyes.

Five

The darkness was dreadful, like the blacking out of her last hope. It pressed in on Megan as the hours of the night passed, revealing with merciless clarity that she was facing a blank. She'd taken a desperate gamble and it had failed, leaving her with no cards left to play.

The revelation of her own sexuality had shattered her, throwing her off balance when she most needed a clear head. She'd never thought of herself as a sensual woman. Her youthful passion for Brian had died quickly under the discovery of his true nature, and the publicists' projection of her as an erotic fantasy had merely amused her. In the year following their separation, all her attention had been claimed by her son and her work, and during her incarceration her rage and bitterness had blotted out any need of physical satisfaction.

Yet all the time the truth had been crouching like a tigress, ready to spring out of the darkness. And the truth was terrible. Her body, so alluring on the surface, so cool inside, could be awakened to flaming life by the touch of just one man. And by a dreadful twist of fate, that one man had turned out to be the one she hated.

She didn't weep. She was past that. But the ache in her breast, that never left her night or day, grew heavier. All that mattered was Tommy and finding a way of getting him back. For that she'd been prepared to pay any price. But she'd fumbled it and lost her chance.

Tommy was with her this minute, as he always was. She closed her eyes and her thoughts dwelled on him lovingly: how it would be when they were together again, what he might look like now; how much they would have to tell each other. But thoughts weren't enough. She needed his physical presence, his smile and the feeling of his arms around her neck. The lack of those things was a never-ending pain, and tonight the pain was greater than ever, for he had never seemed so far away.

Suddenly she opened her eyes, wondering if she was going mad, because for a moment she'd been sure she heard him calling. She sat up in the dark, straining her ears, and heard him again, seeming to come from a long way off. She threw off the bedclothes and hurried out of the room without putting on a robe.

"Mommy. Mommy, where are you?" He sounded lost and frightened, as he'd sometimes done when he had nightmares.

"I'm coming," she called. "Don't be frightened. Mommy's here."

She stumbled down the hallway, seeking him in room after room, until finally she came to a room fitted out for a little boy. In the moonlight she could see that the bedspread was decorated with pictures of racing cars, photographs of football players adorned the walls, and a small teddy bear was perched on the pillow. Suddenly her heart was joyful because the long, lonely separation was over, and she opened her arms to her son. "I'm here," she told him. "Oh, Tommy, its so lovely to see you again."

Daniel didn't know what had awakened him, but he sat up quickly, certain that something was wrong. He was out of bed in a moment, pulling a light robe over his nakedness, and hurrying into the hallway. There he stiffened with shock. The door to his son's room was open, and a voice was coming from inside. He went quietly as far as the door, and there he paused, halted by an instinct for danger that warned him to take the next few steps cautiously. The voice coming from inside was Megan's, saying things that broke Daniel's heart.

"Did you think I wasn't coming back, darling? I know I've been away a long time, but I thought of you every moment. I knew we'd be together again one day. I've missed you so much . . . but now we've found each other at last."

Daniel crept noiselessly into the room. Megan was sitting on the bed, smiling and talking eagerly to someone that only she could see. His first unnerving thought was that she'd lost her wits, his second was that she was trying another trick. But as he grew closer he realized that this was no trick. Daniel had seen sleepwalking before and could recognize the real thing.

Megan's eyes were open, but it was clear that she was oblivious of him. Daniel held his breath lest he make a clumsy move and awaken her abruptly. As he stood, undecided, she began talking to her son again, and Daniel listened, not to the words, but to the aching loneliness that infused them. There was a note in her voice that told him, as nothing else could, the truth about what she'd suffered in the past three years, the distracted misery of separation from a beloved child, a misery that drove out every other thought, and that he understood so well. Now she thought the separation was over, and he dreaded the moment when she must learn the truth.

"Megan." He spoke quietly, leaning down to touch her on the shoulder. "Leave him now. Let him sleep."

She answered without looking at him. "But he can't sleep. He had a nightmare. I heard him calling for me. I've heard him so often...but it was always a dream before." She smiled and the radiance took his breath away. "Now he's really here at last...I want to stay with him...just a little longer—"

Daniel looked around him wildly. He must get her back to bed before she awoke to cruel reality, but he didn't know how. Playing for time, he sat beside her and slipped an arm around her shoulders. "He needs his sleep," he urged. "He's just a little boy."

She spoke wistfully. "He needs his mother. He's been without me for so long. Perhaps he's forgotten me."

"Of course he won't have forgotten you. He loves you."

Her face lit up. "Do you think so? Do you really think so? It's been so long. I wonder what they've told him."

"Does it matter?"

"No, not really. All that matters is that Tommy and I are together again, aren't we, darling?" She appealed to Tommy. "We've got so much to talk about and so much to do—all the things that we used to do together. Do you remember how we loved going to fun fairs? And we'd go on the scenic railway and you held my hand when the big dips came because I was always scared? We're going to find the biggest fun fair in the world... and it'll be just like old times...."

Something seemed to be grasping Daniel's throat and making it ache, and for a moment he couldn't see properly. And then the thing he'd feared happened. A motorbike screamed past in the road outside, making a noise loud enough to awaken the dead. A violent shudder went through Megan, and she turned to stare at Daniel with wild eyes. "It's all right," he said quickly. "I'm here."

Why he should think this might comfort her was later to puzzle him, but he spoke instinctively, and he seemed to be right, for the tension left her face and she didn't protest when he took her hand. "I don't know this room," she said, blinking vaguely. "How did I get here?"

"It's my son's room. You were walking in your sleep," he said gently. "Come on. Let's get you back to bed before you catch cold again." He took hold of her shoulders, but she wouldn't move. "Tommy..." she said desperately. "He was here—"

"Megan, he was only a dream. You were asleep."

"You mean, he was never here at all?" she whispered. "I don't really have him back?" She crossed her arms over her chest and bent her head, rocking back and forth in silent grief.

Her pain seemed to shiver through him unbearably.
If only he could do something, anything, to make
things right for her. "Come along," he said helplessly.
"Come back to bed."

She let him draw her to her feet and lead her away.
She seemed stunned. Once in her room, he urged her
to sit down on the bed, lifted her feet and swung them
around until he could pull the blankets over them.

"I didn't even know I'd gone to sleep," she said
slowly. "I was thinking about Tommy...and then I
heard him call me... It was so clear...but I was just
hallucinating, wasn't I?"

"Not hallucinating, dreaming," he said. "When you
want something very much, it can be so strong that it
seems real."

"Want something very much," she echoed. "Yes,
you could say I want Tommy very much. For three
years I dreamed about nothing else, night and day.
When I knew I was going to be freed I thought I'd see
him again. I knew Brian would fight me about his custody, but I didn't think he'd refuse to even let me see
him. It's become an obsession. I'd do anything—anything..." Her voice trailed away.

Daniel sat down beside her. "Was that what it was
all about?" he asked gently.

"Yes," she admitted wearily, "that's what it was all
about. I want him back so much I just couldn't see
anything else. You don't have to tell me that I behaved
badly—"

"I wasn't going to—"

"I know I did. I tried to use you. You were right, I
was trying to turn you into my instrument, to clear me.
I didn't think about you as a person, or your rights. I
was too desperate to care what I did."

"Would you have gone through with it?" he asked curiously.

"Yes," she said simply.

"With me? Hating me as you do?"

For the first time she looked him in the eye. "With the devil himself if he'd help me get Tommy back," she said. "There, now you know how wicked I can be, and you're disgusted, and you're probably right. I'll be out of here tomorrow."

"Where will you go?"

She shrugged. "Back to the boarding house, I suppose."

Only a few hours ago he'd told himself that he'd enjoy throwing her out, but now he heard himself saying, "You can't go back there."

"I can't stay here," she said stubbornly.

He wasn't by nature a tactful man, but somehow tact came to him now. Or perhaps it was guile. Whatever it was, it was what he needed. "But you don't have to rush off tomorrow morning. Take a couple of days to find something."

She didn't answer him directly. For the first time she seemed to become aware that she was holding a small teddy bear in her hand. "How did I get this?"

"It was in my son's room. You must have thought it was Tommy's."

"I'm sorry." She gave it to him.

"Go back to sleep, Megan."

Daniel crept out and made his way back to the room where he'd found her. He put on a small table lamp at the side of the bed, straightened the bedspread and replaced the teddy bear, adjusting its position twice before he was satisfied. When he was sure everything was as it had been, he looked around him. Normally nobody ever came here but himself. His cleaning woman had strict instructions never to enter. Megan was the first intruder since— His mind always stopped there. Since.

But she didn't feel like an intruder. Her anguish over her son gave them a companionship in grief, even if she didn't know about it, and he didn't resent her presence as he would have resented anyone else's.

He opened a drawer and took out a photograph of a little boy. He was about seven years old, with a cheeky grin, a tooth missing in the middle, and a face full of mischief. Daniel touched the glass over the picture, his fingers straining to find a way through to the child, but there was only coldness. Megan's words echoed through his heart.

How would you know what it's like to lose your child and think about him every moment of every day, becoming obsessed with him?

He could have told her how he knew, if only he could have found the words. But he wasn't used to having to express his deepest feelings. With Sally, it had seldom been necessary. She'd loved him enough to understand the things he couldn't say. But now, no words would come.

And where, in any case, were the words that would describe the little boy full of fun and devilment, yet with a heart that was kind beyond his years? How could any man describe the feel of his son's arms around his neck, and the warmth of his childish, unsentimental love? In agony, Daniel bowed his head over the picture, pressing his lips to the cold glass again and again. But there was no returning embrace, no eager whisper of "I love you, Daddy." And the little boy's shining eyes stared out sightlessly.

* * *

Daniel was out when Megan got up the next morning. She made herself some breakfast and was starting to pour tea when she heard a key in the front door. Assuming it was Daniel, she stayed as she was, to finish pouring, and heard a startled gasp behind her, and a woman saying, "Oh, my Lord!"

Megan turned and saw a plump, elderly woman in a smock, her hand over her heart. "You did give me a start," the woman said. "I thought you were a ghost." She recovered her wits and regarded Megan with suspicion.

"Mr. Keller invited me to stay for a few days," Megan explained. "My name is Megan Anderson."

The woman registered only the barest flicker. Perhaps contact with Daniel had taught her not to be surprised at anything. She went on imperturbably. "I'm Gladys. Yes, I'll have a cup if there's one going. Three sugars, please. I need all my energy for this house." She saw Megan looking at her inquiringly and added, "I 'do' for Mr. Keller. Three afternoons a week. I've been off looking after my sister, who's been poorly. I told Mr. Keller I wouldn't be back until next week, but my sister's better now and I can't stand that idiot she married at any price, so I popped home a bit early." She ran out of breath.

Megan handed her a cup of well-sugared tea. "Why did you think I was a ghost?"

"That sweater, dear. It's like one Sally had—Mrs. Keller. I often saw her standing in this kitchen in it. She used to wear it for working because it's yellow."

"I don't understand...."

"Cheerful, you see. She always liked to be cheerful. She used to laugh and joke all the time. She could even make *him* smile, and that took some doing. Not a naturally cheerful man, Mr. Keller, but he'd smile and laugh for her.''

''What happened to her?''

''Died. She was out in the car with their little boy and another car just smashed into them. It was terrible. I thought he'd go mad.''

''He? You mean, Mr. Keller?''

''That's right. They were everything to him, and all the lights went out for him when it happened. It was two days before Christmas. They had all the decorations up, and the tree, with the presents around it. There was a big box with his gift to her, all shiny wrapped. She kept begging him to tell her what was in it, and he kept teasing her, saying, 'Wait and you'll find out.' Well, she never did find out, poor lass.''

Megan remembered her last Christmas of freedom, the first since the break-up of her marriage. She'd taken Tommy to visit some cousins who had five children of their own, and it had been a happy time. There had been no hint of the horror that was about to fall on them. That horror was Daniel Keller's fault. But somehow it was impossible to hate him when she thought of him alone in this house with the tree and the presents that would never be given. ''It must have made a ghastly mockery to spend Christmas here, with all those happy preparations around him,'' she murmured.

''Oh, but he didn't,'' Gladys said. ''He cleared everything out. The tree, the decorations, presents, turkey—the lot. The house was like a desert. He worked nonstop over that Christmas. I've never seen him smile since. Of course, the little boy—'' She jumped as she heard a key in the lock and went on in a forced voice, "Well, here I am, ready to start work again. Thanks for the tea. I'll get on now."

Daniel appeared in the kitchen doorway. He looked startled to see Gladys. "I'm glad your sister's better," he said when he'd heard her explanation, "but there was no need to hurry back." Megan had the feeling he was annoyed. Gladys seemed to sense it, too, for she scuttled away upstairs. "I'm sorry, I should have warned you she'd be coming," he said. "But I wasn't expecting her back yet."

"It doesn't matter."

"Gladys is a natural born gossip," he said, following some train of thought of his own. "She's a dear soul, but it doesn't do to take every word as gospel."

"She told me about your wife and son. I wish I'd known before. That room I went to last night...it was your son's room, wasn't it? And the teddy bear..."

"Was also his."

She gave a frayed smile. "I'm leaving this morning. You'll be glad to see the back of me."

"I told you last night, take a few days to find somewhere."

But she shook her head. "There isn't anywhere, Daniel. Thank you for protecting me this long, but now I've got to go out to face the world myself."

"And do what? How will you get Tommy back without my help?"

She looked up. "Your help? You'd do that... after what I—?"

"I think we should forget about that," he said quickly. "It didn't happen. The only thing we should think of now is proving your innocence."

"You believe me innocent?" she asked eagerly.

He didn't answer at once. "I guess maybe I do," he said at last.

"You don't sound entirely convinced."

"It's hard to face what I did to you. I don't want to believe you innocent, Megan. It leaves me with too many burdens to carry. But somehow the picture of you as a murderess just doesn't convince me anymore. Maybe it happened last night." He saw her looking at him, and added hastily, "I mean, when you were sleepwalking—the way you talked to that little boy. Even the way you were ready to seduce me to get him back. A woman who would go the lengths of sleeping with a man she hates to be reunited with her son would never do anything that would separate her from him in the first place."

Without warning, remembered sensations streamed through her—the feel of his hand on her breast, hot tremors going through her body, the eager desire to invite him further. *A man she hates*...

She averted her eyes, not to let him see her true feelings. "You're right about one thing," she said. "I wouldn't do anything that could separate me from Tommy, and I didn't kill Grainger."

Daniel took a deep breath. "So we have to do something about it."

Six

Brian Anderson's home was set well back from the road, with a curved drive that swept in one side and out the other. Trees protected the house from the eyes of passersby, and Daniel was well along the driveway before he caught his first sight of the building. It was clearly the dwelling of a wealthy, successful man, one who cared a lot about appearances. Daniel felt his hackles rising fast. There was something about this kind of luxurious, perfectly kept house that had always antagonized him. He tried to ignore the feeling and be impartial, but the memory of Megan in the shabby little apartment where he'd first found her wouldn't go away.

He rang the bell and listened while it sounded deep inside the house. After a moment, the door was opened by a middle-aged woman in a maid's uniform. "I'd like to see Mr. Anderson," Daniel told her.

"Who shall I say?"

"Detective Inspector Daniel Keller."

She looked uncertain. "I'll have to see." She closed the door, leaving him outside. After a moment, she returned. "He says he'll see you."

"Thank you," Daniel said ironically. "That's very gracious of him."

"Yes, it is," she said, unconscious of the irony. "He doesn't see everyone."

She led him into a large, oak-paneled study where Brian Anderson was sitting behind a desk, concentrating on a computer screen. He waited for a precisely calculated ten seconds before looking up, which gave Daniel a chance to consider the room. To one side of the desk was a large photograph of a young woman. She looked in her mid-twenties and was groomed and made up to glossy perfection, but to Daniel's eye her glamor was hard and artificial, and her sexuality seemed calculated and sprayed on. He preferred Megan's beauty with its hint of bruised vulnerability, but evidently Brian Anderson did not. His opinion of the man, not high to start with, sank further.

At last Anderson looked up, stretching his mouth in an approximation of affability that didn't reach his eyes. "Detective Inspector," he said slowly, as if considering the words. "My congratulations."

"Congratulations?"

"Since you announced yourself by your rank I assume you've been reinstated in the force. Isn't that a matter for congratulation?"

"It would be if it had happened," Daniel retorted, cursing himself for clumsiness. The fact was that he already disliked Anderson so much that he'd tried to

intimidate him. But it had backfired, and now he was
at a disadvantage.

Anderson gave a cold smile. "I see. One of those
unconscious slips that we all make sometimes," he
said, leaving Daniel with the conviction that he'd understood only too well. "So you're not back in the
force yet. That means I can offer you a drink. What
will you have?" He moved toward the liquor cabinet.

It was on the tip of Daniel's tongue to say he'd die
before he'd take anything Brian Anderson had to offer, but he remembered in time that he wanted to keep
things cordial, so he forced a smile and said, "Something soft, please. I'm driving."

"And like all good police officers, you disapprove of
drinking and driving."

After a moment, Daniel said, "That's right."

Anderson poured him a lemonade. "Now, what can
I do for you, Detective Inspector?"

There might have been the hint of a sneer on the final two words, but Daniel told himself not to get para-
noid. "I've come about your wife," he said.

"You mean my ex-wife. We've been divorced for
over a year."

"You must still have been delighted at the result of
her appeal," Daniel persisted.

Anderson hesitated. "To be frank, that's a difficult
question to answer."

"Are you telling me it wasn't a relief to know that
she was innocent?"

"But I don't know that," Anderson said blandly.
"She was released . . . but that's not quite the same
thing, is it?"

"The court found that there wasn't enough evidence to convict her. In law, that's innocence."

"Ah, yes, in law. But the law is forced to take a very narrow view. For the rest of us it's a little different."

"Are you saying you believe her guilty?"

"I'd be more interested to know what you believe, Detective Inspector. What is this visit all about? You formed your opinion about Megan three years ago. You must have been very convinced of your case to, er, lose that statement."

Daniel gripped his glass so hard that he had to set it down in case he crushed it. He was swamped by irrational hate toward this man who'd once sworn to love and cherish Megan, and was now so coldly indifferent to her troubles. "You imply that I lost that statement deliberately," he said, keeping calm by an effort of will.

Brian gave a careless, self-confident smile. "Let's just say that I believe those psychologists who tell us that there's no such thing as a genuine accident. All accidents spring from the subconscious."

"This one sprang from exhaustion and overwork," Daniel said firmly. "Policemen make mistakes, too, but ours attract more attention than other people's."

"All right, it was a genuine mistake," Brian said with a shrug. "But what does it prove? That witness saw a woman who could have been anyone."

"I believe he saw Megan," Daniel said emphatically, "and if that's so, she couldn't possibly have killed Henry Grainger."

"So why are you here?" An incredulous smile stretched his thin mouth. "Not an attack of conscience, surely? Acting the social worker?"

"Let's say I'd like to know why you won't take her calls."

"Why should I? What is there to say?"

"There's a lot to say," Daniel said, controlling his temper. "Your wife—your ex-wife—lost everything when she was convicted. Now her conviction's been reversed, she's entitled to some of it back."

"Have I understood you properly?" Anderson asked. "You want me to offer her a reconciliation? Take her back? Is that what *she* wants?"

Suddenly Daniel was gasping for air. Until that moment he'd believed himself dispassionate, in command, but the brutal picture presented by that cool question filled him with revulsion. Megan and this self-satisfied man. Living with him. Letting him touch her. She'd said, "I'll do anything to get Tommy back...the devil himself—" How far would she go? *I'll do anything...*

"I don't...know what she wants," he managed to say.

"But you *are* here on her behalf, aren't you?"

"Only to make you see reason about not shutting her out. She's entitled to see her son."

"She's really got you on her side, hasn't she? A persuasive lady, I have to admit. But you see, I know Megan better than you. Have you discovered yet that she has a killing temper, or has she carefully kept that little tidbit to herself?"

"I've seen her when she was upset," Daniel conceded, remembering how Megan had flown at him on that first evening. "But she has plenty of cause to be upset."

Brian ignored the last part of this remark. "It's a spectacular temper, isn't it?" he asked affably. "Once seen, never forgotten. They didn't call her Tiger Lady for nothing. Henry Grainger should have been more careful."

"Good God!" Daniel exclaimed in disgust. "Do you *want* to think her guilty? What about your son?"

"My son is being protected from her. As a responsible father, I consider that my first duty. Tommy has forgotten Megan very satisfactorily, and I've no intention of allowing his life to be ruined by an unstable woman. And I may as well tell you that I shall soon be marrying again." He nodded in the direction of the picture of the young woman. "My future wife will be an excellent mother to Tommy. If—" He checked himself as the phone rang. "Excuse me." He answered, and Daniel could just hear a female voice through the phone. At once, Anderson's voice altered. "Hello, Selena, sweetheart," he murmured.

Daniel was taken aback by the change that had come over the man. His very skin seemed to be suffused by awareness of the woman he was speaking to. Daniel didn't think it was love he was witnessing. He'd already judged Anderson incapable of a true emotion. But sexually he was in thrall to the brassy creature staring out of the picture. Like a good policeman, Daniel filed the knowledge away for future reference.

Anderson became suddenly self-conscious. "Would you mind waiting outside a moment?" he said abruptly.

Thus dismissed, Daniel went out into the hall and began to look around, taking in the tasteful luxury, the signs of a man who'd been a success in business and was thoroughly satisfied with himself. He'd seldom disliked anyone so much at first acquaintance as he disliked Brian Anderson.

As he could hear that Anderson was settling into a long conversation, he wandered toward the back of the house where he found a room with large windows on

two sides, giving it a sunny aspect. Several pictures
hung on the walls, one of which attracted his attention. It showed a puppy bouncing high in the air after
a ball, and was clearly the work of a very young artist.
But though the execution was immature, the lines were
confident and true, revealing a genuine flair.

There was no sound or movement, but his trained
instincts made him suddenly aware that he was no
longer alone. Turning, he saw a boy of about nine
standing in a door that led out to the garden, watching
him, and he felt a frisson go up his spine at something
familiar about this child. Superficially he didn't re-
semble Megan. His features had the unfinished look
common in young children, and his only resemblance
was to other nine-year-old boys. But this had to be
Megan's son because he had her quality of intense
stillness, like a cat peering through grass. He stood
watching in silence, sizing Daniel up. "Hello," he said
at last. "That's my picture."

"You mean, you painted it?" The child nodded.
"It's excellent. You're very talented."

"It's my puppy, Jacko. I like drawing things that are
alive. It's nice if you can get them looking right." He
added, "I'm Tommy."

Daniel decided to work fast. He wasn't sure how
much time he had. "I guessed you must be," he said.
"You're exactly as your mother described you."

A sudden glow lay on the child's face. "You know
my mother?" he asked eagerly.

So he'd forgotten Megan "very satisfactorily," had
he? Daniel thought grimly. "Yes, I know her," he said.

"Is she coming to see me soon? I thought she'd come
as soon as they let her out—but she didn't."

"You knew she was out?" Daniel asked cautiously.

"One of the boys at school showed me the paper. I didn't know. Daddy just said she'd gone away and left us. He made it sound as if she didn't love me anymore."

"Don't ever believe that," Daniel said at once.

The child shook his head. "I never did," he said with a simple dignity that was far beyond his years. "Daddy was very angry when I found out the truth. He said I shouldn't go back to that school and now I have to go somewhere else, and I don't like it."

"What school do you go to now?" Daniel asked softly.

"Buckbridge Junior."

Daniel sat down so that his face was nearer Tommy's level. "I don't know how much time we have, so listen carefully," he said, and Tommy nodded intently. "Your mother couldn't come to see you because she hasn't been well. But she sent me to talk to your father and . . . and tell you that she still loves you. She thinks about you all the time."

"Then why doesn't she come to see me?"

"She will, just as soon as she can."

"You mean, when Daddy lets her."

It was said with a sad wisdom that was too much for a boy of his age. And before Daniel could suppress it, came the fleeting thought, my fault?

"You miss her a lot, don't you?" he said gently.

Tommy nodded, looking up at him, and Daniel saw that he had Megan's eyes, a brown so light that it was almost golden.

"Look," Tommy said, tugging at Daniel's arm and taking him to a small cupboard, which he pulled open. From inside he took a sketchbook and flipped over some pages until he came to a sketch of a woman's head. Like the picture on the wall, it was rough and immature, but the likeness was there in the angle of the head and the curve of the lips. Daniel felt a pain around his heart at the thought of the lonely child drawing his mother to protect himself from the people who wanted to wipe her from his mind.

"Can I take this?" he asked quickly.

Tommy seemed to understand perfectly because in a moment he'd ripped out the page, folded it and handed it to Daniel. "Will you tell her...tell her..." His voice wobbled.

"Don't worry," Daniel said gently. "This will tell her everything she wants to know. And don't let anyone say she's forgotten you, because she hasn't. She's your mother, and mothers don't forget." Something made him add, "Neither do fathers."

Tommy gave him a puzzled look, but before he could ask anything there was a sound in the hall. Daniel had a sudden inspiration. Pulling out a pen, he scribbled some figures on the pad and closed it, mouthing "Telephone." Tommy looked at him in comprehension. The next moment a shadow darkened the doorway and they both looked up to see an imposing elderly woman with an expression of iron. "I think this conversation has gone far enough," she said in a hard voice.

Tommy was standing close enough for Daniel to feel him flinch. It was obvious who this was. Her resemblance to Brian Anderson was marked, except that she had a more decided chin. She came forward and looked down at Tommy, dominating him.

"What have I told you?" she demanded. When he didn't answer, she repeated firmly, "What have I told you, Tommy? I've told you not to mention that woman in this house. Haven't I?"

"She's not 'that woman,'" Daniel said in disgust. "She's his mother."

He might not have spoken for all the heed she paid him.

"You're normally such a good little boy. It's a shame to spoil it by being disobedient, dwelling on people who are no good and best forgotten. What were you saying?"

Tommy averted his head from them both. Although he couldn't see the child's face, Daniel guessed he was fighting back tears.

"Tommy," Mrs. Anderson's voice was as iron as her face. *"What were you saying?"*

"For God's sake, stop this," Daniel said desperately. "It's sick, trying to force a child to forget his mother."

Mrs. Anderson seemed to become aware of him. "I don't know who you are or what you're doing here, but you certainly have no right to upset the boy by dragging up painful memories."

"If he's upset, it's because he's being bullied by a woman who appears to have the sensitivity of a rhinoceros," Daniel said through gritted teeth.

Tommy made a small choking sound, showing that he'd appreciated this description. Mrs. Anderson looked daggers at him. "That was a very vulgar remark, and you're a very naughty little boy," she said. "What would your new mommy say about your behavior?"

Tommy's mirth vanished, and his face took on a mulish aspect. "She's not my mommy," he said at once. "I don't like her. And she doesn't like me."

"I forbid you to say things like that," his grand-mother said in a hard voice. "You're just a silly little boy. You don't know what you're talking about."

"I know if someone doesn't like me," Tommy said stubbornly. "She calls me 'that brat.'"

"By 'she' I suppose you mean Miss Bracewell. You know your father has told you to call her Mommy."

"But she isn't my mommy," the child repeated, al-most in tears, but refusing to yield.

"What's going on here?" Brian demanded, coming into the room.

"You should be more careful whom you let into the house, Brian," the woman declared loftily. "This man seems to believe he can interfere in what doesn't con-cern him."

"So I've already discovered," Anderson said grimly. "All right, Mother, you can leave Mr. Keller to me. You'd better take Tommy away."

Mrs. Anderson took the child's hand firmly and marched him out of the room, but not before Tommy had turned back and given Daniel a beseeching look. He forced himself to cover his anger with a smile, try-ing to tell the child that he'd see Megan, give her the picture and pass on her son's love. A smile seemed a fragile thing to carry so many burdens.

"I think you'd better leave now," Anderson said dismissively.

"I'll leave, but you haven't heard the last of me."

"Spare me the threats. Tell Megan that for every lawyer she hires, I'll hire ten. I'll blacken her name and keep her tied up in the courts for years. Tommy will be grown up before she ever sets eyes on him again. I hope I make myself clear."

"Perfectly," Daniel said grimly.

"Then I see nothing to keep you here."

He followed Daniel out to his car, and at the last minute he said, "Take this as a friendly warning. Megan is using you. That's her way. She seems sweet and delightful, but underneath it she's a schemer, a user. Somehow I would have expected a man of your experience to have spotted that earlier."

"Good day to you," Daniel snapped, and got into the car. It took all his self-restraint not to sock Brian Anderson in the jaw.

"What did Brian say?" Megan demanded as soon as he got home.

"Just what you expected him to say. No dice. Don't look so cast down. I have something that will please you. Here." He took the picture out of his jacket and offered it to her. "Tommy gave it to me, for you."

Instantly her face was alight. "You saw Tommy?" she asked eagerly.

"I actually had a few minutes alone with him before we were interrupted. Megan, he knows all about it. One of his school friends saw it in the paper and told him."

"He knows I was in prison? Oh, God!"

"He knows you've been cleared. He knows you're free and he longs to see you. He loves you." Daniel was speaking quickly, trying to impress her mind with some good news and drive the sadness from her face. "The others are trying to make him forget you, *but they're failing*. Hold on to that."

He wasn't sure that she heard him. She was staring at the picture. "Tommy did this?" she whispered.

"That's how he keeps your memory alive, despite everything they can do."

"He still loves me, doesn't he?" Her eyes were glowing.

"Yes, he still loves you a lot," Daniel said. Her lightning change from despondency to radiance was giving him a hard time. She'd lost so much, and there was still such a mountain to climb. He didn't know how to tell her that Brian was planning to remarry. He dreaded to see the despair return to her face, and not merely because he felt guilty. This woman's pain was unlike any other's. It had a way of seizing his heart and becoming his own pain. He didn't examine this too closely, or ask why, but it disturbed him. "Listen," he said, "I've discovered something else. Brian has put Tommy in a different school—Buckbridge Junior. Tommy told me that himself."

"I could see him," she cried eagerly. "Let's go now."

"Megan, it's Sunday."

"Tomorrow, then. Just a glimpse. I don't care how far away I am. I must see him. Don't try to stop me."

"I'm not trying to stop you. I'll even take you there."

"When? First thing in the morning?"

"Whenever you like. Megan, calm down."

"How can I calm down when I'm going to see Tommy again? If only I could tell you what it's been like, missing him every moment—thinking of him…"

"You don't have to tell me," he said. "I know how memory can be a blessing and a torment."

"Yes, of course," she said, sobering instantly. He guessed she was thinking of his wife, but it was his son who was in his heart at that moment. There was nothing quite like the love of a child, or the empty ache when his arms no longer went around your neck in eager confirmation of the most spontaneous, uncalculating love of all. If he could have told her his thoughts, they might have drawn close on common ground, but as always, at such moments his tongue seemed to be chained.

Suddenly she smiled at him, and there was a confidence and contentment in that smile that filled him with dread. To fail her now would be the most terrible thing in the world. "Don't build your hopes up," he said. "There are still a lot of hard things ahead of you, and you're going to need all your courage."

"But it can be done, can't it?" she asked eagerly. "I can get Tommy back, can't I?"

He had no idea, but he wasn't strong enough to destroy the fragile hope that was keeping her going. "We can do it," he said at last. "Somehow . . . we're going to do it." He brushed the hair away from her forehead and took her face between his hands. Now, he knew, was the moment to tell her the worst. The words struggled on the edge of his tongue, until at last . . . "We'll find a way," he said gently. "Trust me."

He despised himself as a coward, but he couldn't help it.

They found the school the next morning and waited in Daniel's car, their eyes on the entrance, but it was soon obvious that this would be useless. All they could see was a set of wrought-iron gates through which cars swept every few minutes. There was no hope of recognizing Tommy. Megan stayed calm but her face was dreadfully pale. "Wait here," Daniel told her.

He was gone half an hour, and when he came back, he said, "I've been looking at the playing fields right around the back. There's a wire fence where we can get a good view."

They took up position outside the fence and waited for three hours. During all that time Megan scarcely moved. Her hands rested on the wire, and every time a class appeared for games, they clenched slightly, then relaxed when there was no sign of Tommy. "Perhaps it wasn't such a good idea, after all," Daniel said. "He may not have a games period today. Let's go."

"You go," she said, not taking her eyes from the field. "I'll stay awhile."

"Well, perhaps I'll stay awhile, too," he said casually.

She didn't hear him. Her hands tightened on the wire and he heard her inhale her breath sharply. A crowd of little boys had appeared on the far side of the playing fields, and Megan's eyes were fixed on one of them. "That's him," she whispered. "That's Tommy."

Frowning, Daniel tried to get a better view. At first glance the distance made all the boys look alike. Then he realized that Megan's instinct hadn't erred. After three years, during which Tommy's appearance must have changed, her mother's heart had chosen him at once.

"Surely they'll come a little closer," he murmured, trying to make it happen by sheer force of will. It seemed monstrously cruel that she should have kept so patient and heartbreaking a vigil and have it rewarded in this meager fashion. But soon he realized that the class had settled at the far end of the field, and wouldn't be coming any nearer. Megan didn't speak. Her eyes were fixed on Tommy with a look more piteous than tears, and she never moved them for the next half hour.

And then it was time for the children to go. They began to leave the field, laughing and fooling with each other, eager to get back to a shower and a change of clothes.

All except one.

A little boy had paused, staring down the field at the wire fence. He was totally still, as still as the woman who looked back at him, and their eyes met over the long distance. For a moment it seemed as if he would run toward her, but then the teacher noticed him lagging behind and called him. The next moment he was gone with the rest.

Still Megan didn't move. Her gaze was fixed on the spot where her son had stood watching her, as though she could recreate him through sheer longing. "It was him, wasn't it?" she whispered. "I wasn't fooling myself?"

"No, you weren't fooling yourself," he said gently. "That was the boy I saw the other day."

"And he knew me, didn't he?" she almost pleaded.

"Yes, he knew you. Let's go home now."

She was quiet all the way home, but then she took charge of cooking supper and a wave of euphoria seemed to be buoying her up. "Go into the living room, and I'll bring the coffee in," she told him.

"That meal was a work of art," he said as they settled down.

"I learned cordon bleu to please Brian," she said with a shrug. "It was one of the things he felt was appropriate for his wife. Do you know, I'd almost forgotten that I could cook like that, but suddenly it's all come back to me. So many things are coming back—as if I'd suddenly returned to life. Tommy knew me. After three years, he knew me as easily as I knew him.

Somehow I just know everything's going to be all right."

Something uneasy in his manner seemed to get through to her. "You've been quiet all evening," she said. "What is it? Look, I know I sound crazily optimistic. I know I've got a battle on my hands. Brian isn't going to give up easily, but suddenly I feel strong enough to fight him. In fact, I feel strong enough for anything, and I owe it to you, so don't spoil it by being downcast."

"I don't want to spoil it," he said unhappily, "but it may be even harder than you think. . . ."

She sat down on the sofa beside him and looked searchingly into his face. "What is it, Daniel? Have you been keeping something back?" His silence gave her the answer, and she took hold of him strongly by the shoulders. "It's all right, you can tell me. I'm strong now. I really am."

"All right," he said heavily. "I should have told you before, but I didn't know how. Brian is planning to marry again."

He saw her face go gray and felt the shock shiver through her body. "Megan, it's all right," he said urgently. "We're going to get him back, I promise."

"A stable family home," she whispered. "That's what the court will say—two parents. Or a mother with a cloud over her."

"A mother he loves," Daniel said insistently. "He hates this other woman, I heard him say so. He said he wouldn't accept her as his mommy. Courts listen to children these days. Megan, listen to me, we're not going to give up. *We're going to prove you innocent and get him back.*"

Seven

"We're going to prove you innocent and get Tommy back," Daniel repeated. "Megan, do you hear me?"

She said nothing, but the desperate look in her eyes was both a reproach and an answer. Unable to bear that look, Daniel bent his head and kissed her on the lips, wrapping his arms right around her slim body and holding her close. There was no passion in his embrace, only a desire to comfort and console her with tenderness and warmth. As he kissed her, he continued to murmur, "It'll be all right...I'm going to make it right for you...trust me."

At last he seemed to get through to her. He felt her relax, and began to stroke her hair. He was glad when she buried her face against him so that she couldn't see his expression with its burden of doubt. He'd made promises that he didn't know how to keep, but somehow he must find a way.

Megan lifted her face again. "Daniel..." she whispered.

Her lips were close to his, and suddenly no power on earth could have stopped him from lowering his head and kissing her. He meant it as consolation—at least, so he told himself—but a million years seemed to have passed since their last kiss only a few seconds ago. Everything had changed. Now there was no comfort or contentment, no reassurance, no friendly easing of strain. Daniel's body went rigid with shock at the riotous sensations coursing through it, and for a moment he could do nothing but hold himself motionless while waves of excitement shook him.

He could feel that it was the same with Megan. The slim body in his arms was tense and urgent as the revelation became clear to her, too. They'd trodden this path before and turned back when their passion had shattered against their mutual mistrust. Since then they'd learned about each other, and mistrust was gradually being replaced by a cautious alliance based on respect and affinity of suffering. But what was happening now had nothing to do with respect and everything to do with the burning need of flesh for flesh. This woman, whom he had no right to think of, much less want, had touched off a craving deep within him that was beyond rational thought, and he, who'd survived twelve years on the force by calculating risks, could do nothing but surrender to it helplessly.

Megan had the feeling of being swept away by a whirlwind. Her mind was against this, but her body wanted it. Nothing mattered now except the fact that his mouth was on hers, moving slowly, savoring each sweet caress, lingering, promising. And the skill of his mouth was matched by the skill of his hands. His touch made her light clothing feel like iron barriers, keeping him out when she wanted to invite him in. It was shocking to feel like this, but she couldn't help herself.

Through the roaring of her senses she managed to murmur, "Daniel..."

"Yes," he said hoarsely.

"We shouldn't do this...I know we shouldn't...."

"Then tell me to stop." She looked up at him helplessly, and with a groan he covered her mouth again. "Tell me to stop," he repeated in a voice that was half command, half plea.

"I can't...you know I can't...." Her words were drowned by his lips covering hers, his tongue in her mouth, exploring her with eager anticipation. She was possessed by tremors of pleasure, startling in their intensity. She hadn't known that such sensations could exist, and now she had no choice but to surrender herself to them right up to the end—whatever the end might be. She didn't know what kind of a lover Daniel would be, but suddenly she was desperate to find out. Nothing must stop her now. Nothing *could* stop her now.

With a quick movement she wrenched open the buttons of his shirt and allowed herself the treat of exploring inside. His chest was thick with curly hair that rasped pleasurably against her palm. Beneath it was a firm, muscular torso, hinting at the strength of his whole body, and delights to come. She could feel the vibrations of pleasure shaking him, and the next moment he'd responded in kind, pulling open the buttons of her top and slipping his hand inside to encompass one full breast. She gasped with sheer delight. Every inch of her body was ready for him, longing for him.

She'd half expected Daniel to be a conventional lover, taking her upstairs to make love in bed because that was "the proper place." But he surprised her by tossing some cushions onto the floor before returning to the serious business of undressing her. Her top was tossed aside, followed by her scanty bra, and then there was nothing to stop him loving both bare breasts with hands and lips and tongue.

He pulled her down onto the cushions and began a tender assault on the richness of her body. Sensations flooded Megan as he accepted the invitation in her proud, peaked nipples, and began to tease them with ruthless skill. She'd thought she knew about sex, but now she discovered that the moderate enjoyment she'd experienced before hadn't even been the beginning. Real pleasure was what was happening to her now, this stunning, mind-numbing, overwhelming onslaught of feelings that utterly possessed her.

Even the very word "pleasure," was inadequate to describe what was happening. It was as though the whole world was opening up to her for the first time. Doors swung wide, revealing glorious visions, vistas leading to infinity, sharply brilliant colors. Ripe fruit hung from the trees, flowers blossomed underfoot, and the whole of creation burst with new life, reflecting the awakening that was taking place inside her. This was what life was about, and she'd never known, never even suspected.

She didn't know who'd stripped off Daniel's shirt, but she suspected it was herself, because she was kissing his body hungrily, inhaling his male scent. He felt good to her, his flesh firm beneath her exploring fingers, beneath her searching mouth. Every inch of her was alive and thrumming with desire for the man whose lean body and muscular thighs held such exciting strength. He'd said that he was a plain man, and just now that was what she wanted; raw, forceful, straightforward, driving her to the edge of ecstasy.

"Daniel..." she whispered. *"Daniel..."*

"It's too late to tell me to stop now," he said hoarsely.

"Don't stop... can't wait..." The last words came from her in a gasp as he moved between her legs and entered her in one hard-driving movement. The sound was matched by his groan as she enveloped him with arms and legs and loins. For a few minutes they were both oblivious to everything except the pleasure they were giving each other. By sheer instinct they found themselves moving in perfect harmony, their bodies attuned as though nature had meant it that way from the beginning of time.

Everything she'd thought she knew about herself seemed to fall away, revealing a truth so deep that she'd never suspected it, although it had been plain to strangers. She *was* Tiger Lady. She belonged in the jungle where only the primitive elements counted, because she herself was primitive, made of fire and air, heat and light.

For years she'd told herself that her nickname was only a creation of the publicists, but they'd seen past the surface to her essential nature; smoky, exotic, animalistic. Now there was no more self-delusion. Her sensuality had come racing out of the forests of the night, eyes blazing, soft paws moving silently over the earth, claws barely concealed. It had pounced, it had her in its grip, was shaking her. Convulsions possessed her body, leaving her exhausted, wrung out and blissful. She would never be the same again.

Daniel looked down into her flushed face, seeing the instant reawakening of desire. He was still hard inside her, and he knew that for him, too, this was just the beginning. She'd touched off a deep, physical craving that threatened to be uncontrollable. Was this why he'd instinctively feared her, because of her power to do this to him? But now he knew he had the same power over her. It was there in her large golden eyes in which distant fires burned, inciting him. It was there in the movements of her hips, and the long beautiful legs that were wound around him. She wanted what only he could give her, just as he wanted what only she could give. But she wouldn't plead for it. She preferred to command, just as he did himself, and the result would be an epic power struggle. The thought of the awesome battles that would ensue sent a renewed thrill through his loins and he began to move again, slowly.

At once a soft growl came up from a place deep within her. A contented tigress might have made that sound, and excitement stirred in him again in response. She unwound her legs from around his body and began to thrust her loins forward in strong, leisurely movements. Her hands, which had been around his neck, loosened their grip and she drew them back. There was a superb arrogance in the way she then clasped them behind her own head and lay looking up at Daniel through half-closed eyes. Her gaze challenged him, saying, "So surprise me," and he was avid to meet that challenge.

His strength came surging back as he moved inside her, exerting all his control to make it long, slow and satisfying. She understood his intention and timed her movements to his, reveling in the exquisite pleasure. This time when their climax approached, she had an extraordinary feeling of racing toward the edge of a cliff. The long drop didn't scare her because she could see only air and light. As Daniel drove explosively into her, she launched herself off into space. Then she was spiraling down, crying out with pleasure and relief at the overwhelming sense of freedom. It felt indescribably good and she arched her back, holding him deep within her, wanting it to last forever. When it was over, she could have wept.

She was devastated by enjoyment. This man was so skilled, so vigorous and satisfying, that she felt drained and totally contented. Dimly she recognized that her troubles were as great as ever, but the utter relaxation of her body was a balm that soothed every wound. It might not last, but for the moment she felt physically at peace and able to cope with whatever happened to her.

Daniel was watching each expression that passed over her face, trying vainly to read them all. His own fulfillment had been total. He wanted to rest his head against her breast, to speak to her tenderly, even perhaps lovingly, and then to sleep in her arms. But she was looking at him through her lashes, and it was impossible for him to tell what else, besides physical contentment, there was in that look. "Well?" he asked lightly.

"Well, what?"

"Was it good?" He cursed himself as soon as the words were out. They were stupid, clumsy, arrogant. But a sudden shyness had overtaken him.

His words—no, not his words, his attitude—had the effect of tightening the springs of tension that had begun to uncoil in Megan. Now she remembered that a chasm still yawned between them. They might no longer be enemies, but they were no more than wary comrades, and she'd lowered her guard. He'd seen her out of control, lost in his power. Her common sense told her it was a bad move.

But prison had taught her many things, among them, dissimulation. So she merely sat up. "Of course it was good," she said with a shrug. "I haven't had a man in five years. Anyone would have been good."

With her back to him, she didn't see the sudden strain in his face, as if she'd slapped him. When he spoke again, his voice was expressionless. "Five years? You were only in prison for three."

"And before that I was separated from my husband, so you assume I was promiscuous?"

"I didn't—"

"After I left Brian I lived without a man by choice."

"And . . . before you left him?" It was none of his business, but he couldn't stop himself from asking.

Megan shrugged. "During our last year together we lived under the same roof, but there was nothing between us. You can believe that or not, as you like."

He just stopped himself making a sound of relief. It was irrational to feel such pleasure. What did it matter to him that she'd had the good taste to reject her worthless husband? It might have mattered once, but she'd made it only too clear that nothing had changed between her and himself. They'd succumbed to a moment of physical madness. The minute it was over she hastened to restore the distance between them.

No, not restore: create. The distance she was establishing now was twice what it had been when they'd returned from seeing Tommy. Then there'd been a camaraderie between them, which she now wanted to deny.

A horrible thought occurred to Daniel. Had Megan really succumbed to madness at all? He'd tried to do her a service, and she was grateful. What had seemed to be passion might be no more than a kind of good manners. Now she was delicately letting him know that gratitude only went so far.

He hastily got up and covered himself. The pleasure of being naked with her was gone. Now he felt as if he'd taken advantage of her defenselessness. He cursed himself for being awkward. But it was too late. For a brief moment something had almost flowered between them. But it was gone.

The next morning's mail brought a letter from Mr. Newton, who announced that the negotiations for her compensation were going sufficiently well for him to make her a more generous advance. Attached to the letter was a check for one thousand pounds.

"That's excellent," Daniel said in a toneless voice. "Now you can afford your own place."

"Of course," Megan agreed instantly. "I'm sorry to have imposed on you. You've done a great deal for me, Daniel, but I can manage alone now and—"

"Cut it out," he ordered harshly. "I haven't even started on what I'm going to do. You can't clear this up on your own. You *need* me. Or were you fooling yourself that you don't?"

"No I—I guess I don't understand. Why are you throwing me out?"

"'Throwing you out?'" he echoed, trying to speak lightly and not entirely succeeding. "That's rich, coming from the woman who once said that anyone's house was better than mine. I'm not 'throwing you out,' but for your sake I think it's better if we live apart. What

happened last night . . . shouldn't have happened. And
if you live independently of me it won't happen again."

"I see," she said slowly. "Yes, I see."

He wanted to shout that she didn't see at all.
Through a long sleepless night he'd been tormented by
the thought that he'd traded on her need of him. He
wanted her, but not that way, not in gratitude and de-
pendence, but freely and with a full heart. Already his
body ached for her again, craved to lie with her in joy
and fulfillment, but if that day should come, he wanted
to look into her shining eyes and see a true passion that
matched his own. And when desire was slaked, he
wanted her to nestle against him in blissful contentment, not withdraw, her debts paid. He knew it might
never happen. But he also knew that even to hope for
it he must first send her away.

They found a boarding house for her, a few miles
away. It was run by Mrs. Cooper, a kindly, middle-
aged woman who either didn't recognize Megan or had
the tact to pretend not to. There were three other oc-
cupants—a married couple and Bert, an elderly taxi
driver who came and went at odd hours. He had three
married daughters who all wanted to give him a home,
and who constantly called him up, "fussing," as he put
it. But Bert was a maverick, preferring the independence of a boarding house and his taxi run. Megan
found him friendly and likable.

For the first time since she'd left prison there was
peace. At least, peace of a kind. Nobody troubled her,
and she could lose herself in the anonymity she'd
craved.

But in another sense her peace had been destroyed.
After lying cold and dull for years, her flesh had been

awakened to scorching life. It had tasted unbearable pleasure and now craved it again, but the only man who could work the miracle had sent her away. He'd done so under the guise of protecting her, but Megan guessed the real reason. He was still mistrustful and wanted to free himself from her. She was dangerous to him.

But as she lay awake at night, trying to subdue her body's demands, Daniel's face would come into her mind, not suffused with desire as she'd seen it recently, but sad and gentle as it had been when he'd first rescued her and cared for her. Hating him, she'd hurled his care back in his teeth, but still he'd lavished it on her.

She finally managed to persuade herself that she should call and make sure he was all right. But all she got was his answering machine. The first time it happened she left a message, but the next three times she hung up without saying anything. Like a blow to the stomach, the answer came to her. She'd been dumped. Daniel had decided that she was a nuisance, and he reckoned he would be better off without her. Or perhaps he'd had all he wanted of her, a kind of revenge for the devastation that had happened in his life? Or he'd simply decided she was guilty, after all, and he was getting out in time? Or—?

"Here, snap out of it, luv." Bert's kindly voice broke into her thoughts. "He'll call."

"I beg your pardon." She came back to the present with a jolt. She and Bert were having breakfast alone together.

"I know that look on your face," he went on. "I saw it on my daughters' faces often enough when they were teenagers. Does he or doesn't he?"

"Does he or doesn't he what?" Megan asked cautiously.

Bert winked. "He loves me, he loves me not..." he intoned mischievously. "That's what my lasses were always wondering. But everything worked out for them."

"As you say, your daughters were teenagers," Megan reminded him.

"Aye, but it's the same at any age," he said sagely. "When love gets you, it gets you. My three really suffered, but it was worth it in the end. They've all got their fellers firmly hog-tied and broken spirited." He chuckled. "That's why I steer clear of them. Freedom for me. But I'm different. Most fellers knuckle under in the end. Now this bloke of yours—"

"You've got it wrong, Bert," she interrupted him desperately. "I'm not in love."

"Pull the other one. Your ears shoot out on stalks every time that phone rings. And when it turns out not to be for you, you droop a little."

"Bert! I do *not* droop," she protested, laughing despite her dismay. "You're quite wrong. He's not... we're not... he's more of a kind of legal adviser."

He grinned. "If you say so, luv."

His words had given her a shock. She was all at sea because this was something she'd never gone through as a teenager. At the age when other girls had been longing for the phone to ring, she'd been fending off male interest. No man had ever kept her guessing. Even Brian had danced attendance, calling her regularly, sometimes too often. This was her first experience with what Bert's daughters and other women went through, and she didn't know how to cope with it.

That was all it was, she assured herself. Inexperience. The idea that she was in love with Daniel was ridiculous. Only, why didn't he call?

She returned to the school and went to the same spot where she'd seen Tommy in the distance. A day passed, then another. She refused to go away without seeing him. After two days' lonely vigil he appeared again with his class. This time he looked in her direction almost at once, and her heart leapt as she realized he was looking for her. But then the teacher noticed what was happening and called him away. Megan crept back into the shelter of the trees as the teacher continued to look in her direction, suspicion written all over him. Sadly, Megan departed. Tommy seemed further away than ever now that her one hope had deserted her. Slowly she returned to the boarding house.

As she entered the front door she met Bert just going out. He winked and jerked his head toward the communal sitting room. "I told you he'd turn up trumps," he said.

She didn't waste time disputing his interpretation but ran into the sitting room, her heart beating madly with hope. There was a moment when the man standing in the blinding sun by the window could have been anybody. Then he turned and grinned at her, an almost boyish grin, such as she'd never seen on him before. The next moment she'd thrown herself into his arms, almost weeping with joy.

She felt his firm, vigorous embrace, and perhaps he would have kissed her, but there was the sound of Mrs. Cooper's voice just outside the door, and they drew apart self-consciously. The landlady's head came around the door. "I expect you and your friend would like some tea," she said cheerily. "The kettle's on."

She withdrew before they could answer. Megan looked at Daniel, swept by indescribable feelings. It wasn't possible that she should love him. Too many barriers stood in the way. But the emotions flooding her broke down barriers, sweeping them away like twigs. Bert had known. That nice, uncomplicated man had recognized the truth because he didn't muddle the issue with irrelevancies—like the fact that the two of them had ruined each other's lives.

"Where on earth have you been?" Daniel asked. "I've been gnawing my fingers, waiting for you."

"I went to catch a glimpse of Tommy."

"I should have thought of that. Did you see him?"

"Yes, but only from a long way off. I felt so bad coming home, I thought you'd deserted me."

He looked suddenly self-conscious. "So that was why I got such a welcome?"

His awkwardness communicated itself to her, and she found herself blushing. Tiger Lady, who'd always had men at the snap of her fingers, suddenly didn't know where to look. "You're my only chance, Daniel," she said self-consciously. "Without you, I've no hope."

"Yes," he said. "Yes, I thought that was it. Well then, I may have some good news for you. I haven't been wasting my time or forgetting you—" His gaze seemed to penetrate right into her.

"Daniel, you just vanished from the earth," she burst out. "You weren't there when I called you and you never called me. I didn't know what to think."

"So you thought the worst. Perhaps I shouldn't blame you for that, but we have to start trusting each other, Megan. Otherwise we've no chance of...of making everything right."

" 'Making everything right,' " she echoed, half noting his ambiguous choice of words. That could mean several things. "Daniel, do you think everything will ever be all right again?"

A look she didn't understand briefly touched his face and was gone in a moment before he replied, "Of course, it will. That's what I've been working on these last few days. You couldn't get me because I've been away, working for you."

Before he could say more, Mrs. Cooper came in with a tea tray. It was clear that Bert had been talking to her, because she beamed on them before announcing, "Now I'll just go and leave you two alone. You'll let me know if there's anything you want, won't you?"

They promised her they would, and she crept out, elaborately tactful.

"Daniel, have you turned up something?" Megan begged.

"I might. It's a long shot, but anything's worth a try. Listen, one of the strongest parts of the case against you was that there weren't any other suspects. The only person who stood to gain by Grainger's death was his nephew, Jackson, who inherited a substantial property."

"I was always sure he must have had something to do with it," Megan remembered. "I know he needed money because Grainger told me so. They were always at daggers drawn. Grainger would have willed the property away from his nephew if he could, but it was tied up in a settlement. I heard him gloat about how Jackson would love to see him dead so that he could inherit. He used to say, 'But it'll be a long time yet. I'm as tough as old boots.' "

"Unfortunately for you, Jackson had a cast-iron alibi. He spent the night at his girlfriend's house, and her brother corroborated it."

"They could both have been lying," Megan pointed out.

"Sure, they could. Mary Aylmer might have lied in the hope of marrying a rich man, and her brother could have supported her to get a share of the pickings. But there was no way to shake them—at least, so I thought.

"After you left the house I went through all the statements again with a fine-tooth comb, and something came back to me. About a year ago I was involved in another case, involving a hospital doctor who specialized in spinal problems. He had to prove where he was at a certain time, and he showed me hospital records showing he was on duty during certain hours. Rather indiscreetly he let me see the names of some of his patients. I'm almost certain that one of them was John Baker."

"But wasn't that—?"

"The brother's name is John Baker, and since he fell off a ladder he spends his life in and out of a wheelchair. The point is, if I'm right, he was in hospital on the night he swears he saw Jackson Grainger with his sister."

"But surely—when this happened . . . ?"

"Megan, try to understand," he pleaded, "when a case is over, it's over. You go on to the next case, and the old ones are dead and gone. There was no reason to make a connection. I must have had this buried in my subconscious for a year. The point is, I may not have remembered the right name, or the right date, or it might be a different John Baker. It's a common enough name—"

"But if it's the same one . . ." she broke in eagerly.

"Then we've caught him out in a damaging lie. But it's a big if. There's another thing. Jackson Grainger never married Mrs. Aylmer. It took me a couple of days to track her down. She and her brother are living in the north. That's where I've been, running them to earth."

"But surely he'd have had to marry her to ensure her silence?"

"Not necessarily. She can't implicate him without incriminating herself and her brother. Besides which, she was still married to Mr. Aylmer at the time."

"Daniel," she said desperately, "where does this get us?"

"I'm not sure. It's a gleam of light, but I can't pursue it alone. I need your help. Tell me, did you ever meet either Mary Aylmer or John Baker?"

"No."

"You're sure they never set eyes on you?"

"Quite sure."

"In that case, we may stand a chance. We need to do a bit of searching around their house, and I can't approach them openly because they'd remember me from before."

"You think I can do it? But surely, they'll know me, too?"

"It's a risk, but I think you can get away with it. They never saw you in the flesh. They only know you as Tiger Lady, and even that was three years ago." He searched her face keenly. "And Tiger Lady can be an actress when she has to be. I've been studying those magazine pictures of you. You manage to get a different mood in each one, and you know how to change your looks to get a certain effect. But just how wide is your range? Could you look dull and dreary if you had to?"

"Just watch me," she breathed. "I can do anything I have to. Anything."

"Then here's what we're going to do...."

Eight

John Baker ran a finger along the windowsill and surveyed it in disgust. "That new woman you hired is a slattern," he snapped. "Get rid of her."

"You must be joking," his sister said sourly. "Do you think it's easy to find someone who'll live in and put up with your nasty moods? The word's got around this neighborhood about what you're like. The advertisement had been up in the news agent's window for six weeks before she answered it, and if you think I'm going to—"

"All right, all right. Stop carrying on."

"She may not dust brilliantly but—"

"She doesn't dust at all."

"Give her time, will you? She's only been here three days, and she's got all the other work to do. And even you said that meal with the funny foreign name she cooked was tasty." John Baker grunted, evidently unwilling to be mollified. "Just shut up about her," Mary Aylmer told him. "She's a godsend."

"You mean she lets you lie around with your feet up," he jeered.

"Well, I'm entitled to put my feet up after looking after you," Mary told him crossly. "It's no picnic being stuck in this house with a moaning so-and-so and not enough money to live on."

"Well, you should have played your cards a bit better, shouldn't you?" he told her nastily.

"Don't start that again."

"Start it *again?* I never stop thinking of it. You had a gold mine there for the taking, and you let it slip through your fingers."

"It wasn't there for the taking," Mary Aylmer said, speaking wearily because they'd had this conversation a thousand times. "It was all a con. He was using us. Anyway, he sends us money regularly."

"Every three months," Baker sneered.

"Well, every three months is regularly."

"Hah! You call that money? A damned pittance. It's nothing to what should have been yours—" He broke off because his sister had given him a warning look.

"What is it, Lily?" she asked sharply of the woman who'd appeared in the doorway.

It was hard to tell how much, if anything, Lily Harper had overheard, or what she'd made of it. Sometimes it seemed impossible that intelligence could live behind those blank eyes and lifeless face. "Do you want the tea now?" she asked after a pause during which she seemed to be trying to remember what she'd been going to say.

"Yes, bring it in here," Mary said.

"And take that fag out of your mouth," Baker shouted at her. "How many times do I have to tell you? Filthy habit."

"Sorry." Lily Harper stubbed out her cigarette, but even as she moved away her hand was reaching for another one.

"Dear God!" Baker muttered. "Is that the best you can get?"

Mary was too fed up to answer him. Instead she got up and went out into the kitchen where Lily was clattering teacups. "I swear I'll do that miserable so-and-so an injury one of these days," she said bitterly.

"You should get out more," Lily ventured.

"How can I? He can't manage for himself."

"I'm here."

Mary's eyes lit up with hope. "You'd look after him for me, just for an evening?"

"Don't mind," Lily said. Nobody could have told from her voice whether she was resigned or enthusiastic, and her features were unrevealing, being mostly hidden behind a curtain of mousy hair that swung around them. Mary had gotten little impression of Lily's face beyond the fact that she slapped on makeup far too heavily without making much improvement.

"Tonight?" Mary said. "Just to let me have a few hours in the pub."

"You go on. I'll manage."

As soon as the evening meal was over, Mary wasted no time in escaping from the house. Lily concentrated on washing up until a slight tap on the kitchen window made her move cautiously toward the back door and open it a crack. A man slipped noiselessly inside and mouthed "Any luck?"

"She keeps everything in a desk in the back room," came the whispered reply. "But it's locked, and the key's on her key ring."

"Don't worry. I'm not a policeman for nothing. I was taught to pick locks by Jake the Snake."

"Jake the Snake?"

"The best in the business—before I put him inside. Show me the way."

While her visitor got to work, Lily put into action a plan of her own. Slipping up to her room, she came down again with a bottle of whiskey and a glass, and proceeded to pour herself a measure, letting them chink together a good deal. After a while she was rewarded.

"Lily, come in here," Baker yelled. She went into the downstairs room where he was watching television, still holding the bottle and glass, and he eyed her nastily. "Are you stealing my whiskey?"

She considered the glass for a long while before answering. "No, Mr. Baker. This is mine."

"Are you sure?"

"I keep a little by me for when I'm feeling low," Lily explained sadly.

"Feeling low," Baker scoffed. "What would you know about that?"

"We all have our crosses to bear," Lily confided. "When I think of mine I just need a little sip to set me up again." Her stupid face brightened. "Would you like some?" She held up the bottle so that he could see the label and appreciate that it was a superior make.

"Don't mind if I do," he growled. "How the hell can you afford a brand like that?"

"It's the only treat I allow myself," Lily informed him mournfully. She poured him a generous measure and set the glass beside him. Baker drained it quickly and held up the glass, which she refilled without protest. Nobody could have told from her impassive manner that she'd already seen this man the worse for wear and knew how little alcohol it took to make it happen. "We all suffer in our own way, Mr. Baker. I expect you suffer, having to live in that wheelchair."

"Terrible," he confirmed, draining the glass again. "I'm a hero, you know. I got like this saving a child's life."

Not by so much as a blink did Lily betray knowledge of a fall from a ladder. "That's very brave of you, Mr. Baker."

"There was talk of awarding me a medal, but nothing came of it. I've always been unlucky, Lily."

"Some of us are. If I had my rights I'd be a rich woman. As it is…" Lily roused herself so far as to give a shrug.

"Rights?" Baker growled in a voice that was already becoming slurred. "Hah! Nobody's been cheated of their rights the way I have."

Lily refilled his glass and settled herself nearby. "Tell me about it, Mr. Baker," she invited.

"You took a helluva risk," Daniel said as they drove south later that night.

"Nothing ventured, nothing gained," Megan said. She tried to speak casually, but in truth she was walking on air.

Daniel heard the exhilarated note in her voice and tried to bring her back to earth. "What exactly did he say?" he asked. "Did he actually admit he'd lied to get Grainger off the hook?"

"Not in so many words," Megan admitted. "But he said he'd 'taken a risk for a friend' who'd turned

around and betrayed him. 'Palmed him off with four-
pence' he said. That's good enough for me.''

"For me, too,'' Daniel agreed. "But not for the
court.''

"All right, what did you get? Was he in the hospital
at the relevant time?''

"I couldn't find that out for sure, I'm afraid.''

"Oh, God!'' In an instant Megan came crashing
down from the heights.

"Wait, don't despair. I did find a letter from that
particular hospital, which makes it clear he's been
treated there at some time, so it's a fair bet that he's the
patient mentioned in those notes. Which means it can
be proved with a little further investigation. And I
found something else. Someone's been paying five
hundred pounds into Mary Aylmer's bank account
every three months.''

"I could have told you that,'' Megan said. "I heard
them talking about it.''

"But I've got the account number and the dates the
payments were made. If it ties up with Jackson Grainger's account, I think we're on our way.''

"'We're on our way,''' she repeated. "We're on our
way.''

"Megan, don't raise your hopes too high,'' he
pleaded. "It's a start, but only a start.''

"All right, I'll try to be realistic, but you don't know
how it makes me feel to have done something positive
after three years staring at walls.'' Megan gave a wry
smile. "It was a relief to get rid of that awful wig, and
it was even nicer to scrape that thick gunge off my
face.''

"I nearly didn't recognize you,'' Daniel said, grin-
ning, "not just because of the wig and thick makeup,

but those shapeless clothes and down-at-the-heel shoes.''

Megan laughed and stuffed the wig into her bag. "Lily Harper, R.I.P.,'' she said triumphantly.

She dozed for an hour and awoke when they were on the outskirts of London. "Feel better?'' Daniel asked.

"Much better, thank you.''

"I'll have you home soon, although it might be an idea—'' Daniel broke off suddenly, cursing under his breath. Looking ahead, Megan saw what had startled him. Another car was coming straight for them on the same side of the road, its headlights almost blinding them as it weaved violently about....

Daniel reacted with the speed and skill of a police driver, swerving into the opposing lane just in time to avoid a collision. For a terrifying second they were directly in the path of a truck, then he swerved back onto his own side of the road. There was a grinding sound as he clipped the car that had been heading for them, and the next moment they shuddered to a standstill.

Megan released her breath. Looking back, she could see that the car had slid into a ditch at the side of the road, and Daniel was sprinting toward it. She hurried out and caught up as Daniel yanked open the door. "What the hell do you think you're...?'' His voice died. Megan saw a deathly pallor come over his face and the next moment he reached inside and hauled out the man behind the wheel, thrusting him back against the car to steady him. The man could hardly stand.

"He's drunk!'' Megan exclaimed.

"Of course he's drunk,'' Daniel snapped in a voice full of murderous contempt. "He thinks it's clever to drink himself silly and get behind the wheel, don't you? *Don't you?*'' He was shaking the man like a rat.

"That's your idea of fun, and if anyone gets in your way that's their hard luck, *isn't it?*"

The other driver stared at him stupidly, but after a moment the shaking he was receiving seemed to clear his head and recognition dawned in his eyes, followed by alarm.

"Yes, you know me," Daniel grated, "and you're scared of me, aren't you? And you're right to be scared. They stopped me getting to you three years ago, but there's nobody to stop me now."

The man mumbled something out of which Megan could only discern the word "accident."

"It wasn't an accident, it was murder," Daniel raged. "You didn't care who you hurt, you just wanted to impress your lady friend. She wasn't concerned about your victims any more than you." He slammed the drunkard back against the car. His head lolled and Daniel steadied it by holding on to it. Suddenly Megan was afraid. Daniel's hands were dreadfully near the man's throat, and they were shaking with the violence of his emotion.

"Daniel," she said quickly, "this is a busy road, and we shouldn't leave your car parked where it is." When he didn't answer, she touched him. *"Daniel!"*

Slowly he turned his head, seeming to notice her for the first time, and Megan gasped at what she saw in his face that burned in his eyes. For a tense moment he didn't move, and she could hear her own heart beating with dread. She didn't understand what was happening here, except that it was like being caught up in a nightmare. She knew the feeling well from her past, but this time it was *his* nightmare. "Daniel," she said again, more gently.

At last he nodded and something terrible died out of his eyes. He calmed himself down with an obvious effort and dropped his hands. The driver, who'd also apparently seen the danger, clasped his throat in relief. But his relief was short-lived. Daniel began to frogmarch him toward his own car.

"Hey," he protested tipsily.

"Shut up," Daniel told him grimly. "You're coming with me." He turned to Megan. "Lock his car and bring the keys with you," he said tersely.

He'd spoken as if to a subordinate on the force, and although he'd regained command of himself it was clear he was still suffering some violent inner turmoil in which Megan barely existed. She did as he wished, knowing that this wasn't the time to demand explanations. Daniel shoved the man into the backseat of his car and when he and Megan were inside, he snapped the lock by the driver's seat that secured all the doors, thus preventing his prisoner from escaping. He hunted for the car phone that had been knocked to the floor by the collision, but when he tried to punch out a number, nothing happened. "Dead," he said in disgust. "All right, we'll just go straight there."

"Go where?" the drunkard demanded.

"Shut up," Daniel told him with a savage look that silenced the man more effectively than words.

On the journey Daniel spoke only once, when he said to Megan, "You're a witness. You saw what he did and the state he's in."

"Yes."

"Good." He relapsed into black silence.

Ten minutes' drive brought them to a police station. Megan glanced at it with a shudder, but it wasn't the same one where she'd once been interrogated, and after a moment she was able to subdue her reaction. Daniel hauled the man out and bundled him unceremoniously into the station, ignoring his faint protest.

The sergeant on the desk looked up in surprise as Daniel marched his prisoner in. "This disgusting object," he declared curtly, "is Carter Denroy, who's drunk out of his mind, and was driving his car on the wrong side of the road. By the grace of God, there wasn't an accident."

"I see," the sergeant said, looking Denroy up and down and taking in his condition. "Well, let's do some tests and see how far over the limit he is."

"And then throw the book at him," Daniel snapped. "It's not the first time. Three years ago he got behind the wheel while he was as drunk as he is now. Only that time God was less merciful, and Denroy ploughed into a car containing Mrs. Sally Keller and her son. His lawyer persuaded the court that it was an aberration, the first and last time he'd ever done such a thing, and he got off with a fine and a suspended sentence." His voice was bitter. "That's how easy it is to kill someone and get away with it."

"Here..." Denroy began to protest, but his voice died away as Daniel look at him again.

The sergeant regarded Daniel with new interest. "It's Detective Inspector Keller, isn't it?" he said. "We worked at the same station once, for about six months. Sergeant Gladstone."

Daniel nodded. "I remember you. Good evening, Sergeant. Can we get on with it?"

Denroy was hurried away. A young constable ushered them into the depths of the station and declared himself ready to take their statements. Megan tried to concentrate, but her mind was seething with what she'd heard.

She'd known that Daniel's wife and son had been killed three years earlier, just before her own arrest. But somehow it had slipped to the back of her mind and she'd never fully examined the implications. Tonight's events had made it real, immediate.

Three years ago Daniel's life had been contented, happy, just like her own. Then misfortune had sprung on them both like a cat out of the jungle. Teeth had ripped up their lives and spat them out in raw, agonized chunks. Ruthless claws had torn the happiness to shreds. For him as for her. Three years ago. *Three years ago.*

"Fine, that's all I need." Megan came out of her reverie to realize that the sergeant was speaking to her. She'd given her statement from the surface of her mind, hardly knowing what she'd said.

Daniel took her arm and together they left the station. He looked different to her. There'd been a terrible hardness about him while he'd dealt with Denroy and gave his statement. It was there still, shading into a bitter exultancy that she understood. It mirrored her own triumph when she'd learned that he'd been suspended from the force. It had seemed a just and righteous feeling at the time, but seeing it in him, she felt uneasy, both about him and about herself.

When they were in the car, he said, "Heaven knows what that respectable boarding house is going to think about the time I get you back there."

"I don't want to go back there tonight," Megan said.

"What?"

"I want to go home with you. There are things we must talk about."

At once he was wary. "Not tonight, Megan."

"Yes, tonight. It's important, Daniel. You know it is."

He didn't ask what she meant, but turned the car in the direction of his home.

Nine

When they were inside the house, Daniel said, "What is it, Megan? What's on your mind?"

"Daniel, I want you to do something for me, without asking why."

"All right," he said, but his voice was guarded.

"I want you to let me interview you."

"What?"

"The way you interviewed me."

"What's going on in your head, Megan?"

"Please, Daniel, just do as I ask."

"But why?"

"Because there are things about you I must know—about Carter Denroy."

She saw his face close against her. "There's no need for that."

"There's every need. Who gave you the right to

know the details of *my* life while keeping your own a
secret?"

"That's different. I have to know about you. It's
part of the case. What happened to me—" a tremor
went through him, "—doesn't come into it."

She looked at him. "Doesn't it? Are you sure about
that?"

His eyes fell first. Her clear, searching gaze seemed
to bore straight into his soul, uncovering places he'd
kept protected from the world. "Never mind," he said,
turning away.

"I mind very much. I think it matters." She put a
gentle hand on his arm and turned him back. "Please,
Daniel, talk to me."

"Will it help us nail Jackson Grainger?"

"That's not what I'm thinking of."

He didn't answer, but he offered no resistance when
she urged him into a chair and sat opposite him. "This
is your interview," he said. "I take it you want to ask
questions?"

"Yes. I want to know about..." She hesitated before taking her courage in both hands. "About Mrs.
Sally Keller."

For a long moment he was silent. When at last he
began to talk, he didn't look at her, but at a point over
her shoulder. "We were married for seven years. We
had a son called Neil, whom we both loved very much.
We loved each other very much, too."

"What sort of a person was she?"

"She was sweet and gentle, and full of generosity. I
was a bit of a tearaway when we met. We were both of
us just kids, and I could have ended up on either side
of the law. All I cared about was getting my kicks out
of life. But then I began to care for her, too, and she

made it plain that if I wanted her, I'd have to straighten myself out. So I did. I pulled myself together, got into the police, and waited three years to marry her.''

"She must have been quite a person," Megan breathed.

"She was my salvation," Daniel said simply.

Megan was silent, trying to cope with the sensations that possessed her at the fervent intensity of that statement. Just as she'd learned only recently what it was like to wait for a phone call that didn't come, so now she was discovering jealousy. Daniel's few words had conjured up a whole world—a world that contained himself, his wife and their son, and that excluded her. Three years after her death Sally still had the power to bring a glow to her husband's eyes, a warmth to his voice. And Megan was jealous.

But Tiger Lady's jungle powers were useless now. Her claws could only damage the delicate fabric of the relationship that was growing between herself and this man. So she kept her feelings to herself, and said only, "And you were happy." It was a statement, not a question.

"I didn't know what it was like to be happy until we were married. I thought I had everything a man could want. Only then, Neil was born, and I discovered there was more." He fell silent. He was still looking past Megan, and he seemed to have forgotten her. A reminiscent half smile touched his mouth, as if he could see something hidden from her. She resisted the temptation to look behind her to see if his wife and son were standing there. There was no need. For Daniel, they *were* there, conjured up by the power of his love. Megan's jealousy flickered again. What sort of woman could wring a man's heart with such yearning, bittersweet memory? What sort of love was it they had known?

"And then?" she prompted at last. Part of her was reluctant to speak, but she had to know.

"And then . . . she took Neil to visit her parents for a weekend. She drove back on Sunday evening. I was expecting her about nine o'clock—but she didn't arrive. At ten I called her parents, but they said she'd left early. Then one of my colleagues from the station turned up on my doorstep. They'd been called out to a fatal accident . . . and he'd recognized her." He stopped.

"Go on," Megan said, gently but persistently.

"The car was a write-off. It had taken three hours for them both to be cut free. When I went to identify her, I hardly knew her—" He broke off and closed his eyes. "She'd always been so full of life, and now she was cold and still—not like my Sally at all. And Neil—he was a real boy, full of bounce, and noise and mischief. Suddenly he was so silent—"

"And Carter Denroy did that?"

Daniel bowed his head. "Yes."

"Did you see him that day?"

He opened his eyes again and spoke in a hard voice. "He was at the station. He'd sobered up by then and was refusing to say anything. The woman with him did all the talking. She kept saying they wanted a lawyer and weren't going to talk until they had one. He was shivering, but she was very cool and collected. Her only thought was how best to manage the situation and extricate themselves. Denroy was a weakling. She knew it, too. She kept giving him little glances of contempt even while she protected him."

"What was she like?" Megan asked in a voice that gave nothing away.

"I've told you—"

"I mean, what did she look like?"

"She was a glamour puss, done up to the nines, face made up to kill."

"Like me, in fact, the first time you saw me?" She spoke so casually that for a moment the force of her remark didn't impress Daniel. But when it did, he turned horror-filled eyes on her. Horror at her implication. Horror at hearing his own half-suspected prejudice dragged out into the open.

She was merciful. She didn't insist on an answer, but continued, "It was just before Christmas, wasn't it? Gladys told me. She said you went straight back to work."

"I couldn't face this house. I turned to my work to save my sanity."

She took a deep breath. "Tell me about that work."

"What?" He stared at her.

"Tell me about your cases then. What were they?"

"How can I remember after all this time?"

"Can you remember *anything* you did then, Daniel?"

He saw where she was leading. Dumbly he shook his head. His eyes were desperate.

"Perhaps you should have taken some time off," she suggested gently.

"That's what Canvey said—in fact several people— but it's the way I was raised. You didn't give in. That was what being a man meant—you didn't give in. You were hard and stoical, and didn't let the world see you were hurting. Time off was for wimps." A shudder went through him. "I believed I was being strong. I never thought—" He couldn't bear to go on.

"It was about then that...that we met," Megan said carefully. She knew she must tread carefully from now on.

But Daniel had the courage not to shy away. "It was then that I took on the Grainger case," he said. "I thought I was in control. It seemed so simple—" He came to a halt, but Megan was too wise to speak. She was holding her breath.

At last he repeated, "I thought I was in control. I know now I was deluding myself. Canvey tried to warn me. He said I used to stare into space, and when someone spoke to me it was like I was coming around from a trance. I didn't believe him. You see, I had no recollection ... I don't know why it never occurred to me that I might harm an innocent person, but it didn't. I was so stupid, so self-satisfied, so damn sure that I was being strong and rising above everything ... and ... and *you* paid the price."

He dropped his head into his hands. Shattered, Megan watched him, aching to comfort him yet knowing the moment hadn't yet arrived. She ventured to stroke his hair, very gently, but she was holding her breath. There was more to come, and she must be patient.

Still with his head bowed, not looking at her, Daniel said, "When someone gave me that statement, I must have put it away to be studied later, and then forgotten all about it. Even now I can't remember it. I wrote something on it—the handwriting is mine—but I have no memory... I didn't frame you Megan, not deliberately. But I wronged you just the same, by being arrogant and self-absorbed, and so convinced that I was infallible that I never thought what I was doing... Oh, God. *Oh, God.*"

A sob tore through his great frame. Without raising his head, he reached out blindly for her, and she enfolded him in her arms. It was the embrace of a mother as much as a lover, enveloping, protective, offering him a place to hide. While his shoulders shook, she kissed and caressed him, seeing again in her mind the way he'd looked three years ago. His face had been pale and livid, the face of a man who was dead, yet still walking. How much had he had to suppress simply to function at all? And all the time the things he'd suppressed seethed and gnawed away inside him, making him a little mad.

He'd made a terrible mistake and she'd paid a terrible price for it, but the mistake had come out of his agony. For three years she'd seen only her own suffering. She didn't blame herself for that. She'd had little else to think of. But now she was presented with *his* suffering, and it appalled her.

"Daniel," she whispered. "Daniel, it's all right...truly it is."

But he didn't hear her. "Forgive me," he choked. "Try to forgive me if you can."

"Yes," she said urgently. "Yes, yes, my love, I forgive you. *Yes*. We'll make everything come right."

He raised his head to look up at her, and his face was wet. He looked desperate, as if he'd been fending off an enemy for years, and that enemy had finally broken through, crushing and defeating him. Now he was as totally defenseless as she'd once longed to see him. She could say and do anything to him, accuse him of any wickedness, hurl any insult, and he would believe her and slip a little further down into hell. It was what she'd once wanted. But not anymore.

She took his face between her two hands, looking down intently into his eyes. "Listen to me," she said fiercely. "It's over. We've got to stop living in the past and tormenting ourselves and each other about our mistakes."

"Say you forgive me," he pleaded.

"I forgive you. It's over."

But she could tell that her words didn't help him. They were, after all, only words, and it would take more than that to give him peace. Slowly Megan leaned down and began to kiss his face. She covered it with small, gentle kisses; his mouth, his eyes. She could feel the tension in his body through her own pressed against it. Gradually Daniel seemed to divine the message of warmth and loving reassurance she was trying to convey. He placed his hands tentatively on her waist and drew her closer yet.

"Megan," he whispered, "I don't deserve this."

"Yes, you do," she whispered back. "You deserve all my best ... my love ..."

She didn't know whether she was calling him her love or saying that he deserved her love. It didn't matter. Both were true. Everything in her was concentrated on this one man and his grief. She kissed him repeatedly. With her lips still on his, she dropped her hands and began to run them over his shoulders, his arms, his chest. Comfort was shading into excitement at the thought that he could be hers again.

But he understood her intention and stopped her. "I swore this wouldn't happen again," he said huskily. "For your sake ... you're too vulnerable."

"Not anymore," she said against his lips. "It isn't me who's vulnerable now. Don't fight it, Daniel. Let me give you everything I have to give. It's the only way I can say... what I want to."

In answer, Daniel tightened his arms and buried his face against her in the action of a man coming home. He stayed like that for a moment, trying to believe that this miracle was really happening. The scent of her warm, sweet body was in his nostrils. It was the scent of desire, of a woman's passion stirring in response to one man, and it called forth his own desire for her, which was never far below the surface. He was possessed by feelings such as he'd never thought to experience, feelings of need and longing so strong that they were indistinguishable from love.

He felt her move, and he drew back, releasing her from his embrace. She took his hand and drew him to his feet. "Come with me," she whispered.

She took him to what had been her bedroom, closed the door behind them, and kissed him softly on the mouth. She began to remove her clothes, but not feverishly as though the need of their flesh was all that mattered, or slowly, as if she meant to tease him. He knew already that what was happening went too deep for that. She did it with a kind of intent simplicity, seeming to have her mind fixed on something that could only be achieved in this way. Daniel watched with wonder as her slim, beautiful body was revealed, offered to him gently and with a graciousness that signified more than passion.

He followed her lead, understanding that it was only when they were naked together that they could communicate. When flesh lay against flesh, skin against skin, warmth against warmth, they would find a truth deeper than words.

He took her into his arms, and she pressed her body against the length of his. He could feel her eager trembling, sense the heartfelt gladness of her response. His manhood was hard and powerful, wanting her, but he waited, leaving the initiative with her, knowing he could trust her for everything.

Her kiss was a promise of peace, calming him even while it enticed him. He accepted the invitation of her mouth, sliding his tongue between her lips to venture into the sweet darkness within. It would be so easy to lose himself in her, trust everything to her. All his life and his training was against such surrender, but now he seemed to have no resistance, and moreover he'd learned to mistrust his own apparent strength, seeing it as a trap and a delusion.

He understood that Megan's strength was the only kind that counted, the strength to forgive a hideous wrong from the depths of a full and courageous heart. True strength lay in soft arms around his neck, sweet lips pressed to his, and a gentle hand leading him to bed.

Moonlight shone through the branches of trees, then through the window, dappling her body with strange jungle shadows. He resisted the urgency of his desire to simply lie there and adore her with his eyes, and his hands, tracing a line from her throat, over the swell of her breast and down to the curve of her hip. She watched him in return, with a look that he could almost have sworn was love, if he hadn't known that to be impossible. She'd called him "my love," and yet...

Why should this woman love him, the man whose carelessness and arrogance had damaged her so terribly? There was no reason except her generosity and the compassion born out of her own suffering. Even as he tried to convince himself, he knew that her love was what he wanted more than anything else on earth. There was only one other thing that he wanted as much, a secret that so far he'd concealed even from her. But he never allowed himself to dwell on it, lest he go mad.

Reverently he bent his head and began to trace patterns with his tongue on her breast. The skin was warm and delicately scented, and he inhaled its fragrance with delight. He could hear the slow, soft throbbing of her heart, with its message of eager anticipation. She didn't move, but her breathing grew deeper as he homed in on the proud nipple and enclosed it between his lips. She gave a long sigh and twined her fingers caressingly in his hair, abandoning herself to the joy of perfect physical love.

Megan lay back, allowing him to tease both nipples to peaks, reveling in the sensations he could give her, sensations that blotted out awareness of all else and made her one concentrated point of pleasure. Warmth and excitement streamed through her body, slowing her heartbeat to an insistent, thunderous rhythm, making her tense with excitement. She watched Daniel through half-closed lids, taking loving note of every movement he made. Her body was ready for him, but more importantly, her heart was ready. With new wisdom she could see that she'd never truly loved a man before. Now the whole magical experience was opening before her, and she went to meet it eagerly.

Then it happened, the thing they'd both been waiting for. Tiger's eyes glowed, her hot breath scorched him, and her catlike sensuality enveloped them both. In the forests of the night they sought and found each other, and their mating was splendid. There was passion and physical abandon, but also tenderness and poetry. She breathed his name as he entered her, and whispered it again as she felt the powerful movements back and forth, driving her to the edge of ecstasy. She could say nothing else, just his name over and over, because that was all there was in the world. *Daniel... Daniel...* on and on in a raging forest fire of pleasure that felt as if it would last forever.

But it exploded at last, engulfing her in flames. They reached their moment together and clung to each other as they fell deeper into the heart of the fire.

And then there was no fire. It was gone, dead, and all they had left was what was in their hearts. It was a moment that destroyed many couples with only physical passion to sustain them, but these two faced it unafraid. And the things that had been there before— compassion, pity, fellowship of suffering, tenderness, the revelations of their own and each other's true natures, the incredulous dawning of love—all these things were there still, with their promise for another day, another night.

Ten

The next day Daniel set about tracing details of bank accounts to see if he could get the elusive piece of evidence that would nail Jackson Grainger. Megan couldn't follow him here, but they met in the evening. She looked strained. "What's happened?" he asked gently.

"I went back to the school, hoping for another look at Tommy today," she said bleakly. "But I couldn't get near. That approach to the playing fields has been fenced off. A passerby told me it was done recently as a safety measure, because someone had seen 'loiterers.'"

Daniel grimaced. "Meaning us."

"Yes. Daniel, are you getting anywhere? *Please* say you are."

"The man who can help me wasn't there today, but he'll be back tomorrow. I'm doing my best, Megan."

"Yes, I know you are." She tried to smile, but it was a painful effort. The euphoria that had gripped her after her success as Lily Harper had evaporated, and now he could see that she was coming close to snapping under the strain. He wished he could take her home with him and love her cares away. He longed to do for her what she'd done for him, offering him the solace of desire fulfilled. It had meant so much to him at the time, and it had been easy to believe that she intended something more than simply comfort. But with the dawn, his doubts had returned. What he'd hoped was love was simply the overflowing of her bountiful nature.

Now it was finished, and he could see she wanted to be alone tonight. He drove her home, kissed her cheek, and watched as she went into the house.

As he was about to drive away he became aware of an elderly man at the wheel of a taxi that had just pulled up. The man was staring at him with curious intentness. Daniel shrugged and drove away.

The next day he went in search of his contact, and this time he found him. When he'd explained what he wanted, the man grunted. "Are you trying to put me back in jail?"

"Nobody will ever know," Daniel promised. "Come on, Joe, you owe me a favor."

"Yeah, all right. If you hadn't spoken up at my trial I'd have gone down for twice as long. Leave it with me, and I'll call you."

He returned home, trying not to let himself hope for too much, but his heart felt that no price would be too great to see Megan happy. The house seemed terribly quiet without her. She'd been there for such a short time, but now her atmosphere lingered in every quiet corner, and he ached for the lack of her.

As he was thinking of throwing together some supper, there was a knock at his front door. He rose quickly, wishing his heart wouldn't beat so urgently. But when he pulled open the door, it wasn't Megan who stood there, but the last person in the world he'd expected to see.

"Tommy."

The little boy on his front step was clutching a bag. He'd set his face into a mask of stubborn determination, but years in the force had taught Daniel to ignore masks and study eyes, and Tommy's eyes were scared, unhappy and desperate. "I—I'm sorry to bother you, Mr. Keller," he began, "b-but . . ."

"Come in." Daniel almost pulled him into the house and shut the front door quickly, after a hasty glance up and down the street. He took Tommy into the kitchen, and the little boy sat down. "Can I see Mommy?" he asked eagerly.

"Tommy, I'm sorry, she doesn't live here."

"But you know where she is, don't you? You could call her?"

"Right now," Daniel said, reaching for the kitchen phone, praying to find Megan at home.

The landlady answered, and went off to find her. After a few nail-biting moments he heard Megan's voice. "Get over here quickly," he urged. "Tommy's arrived. He came looking for you."

He heard her gasp of joy, then the whispered, "I'm coming, I'm coming." The line went dead.

"She's on her way," Daniel told Tommy. "How did you know to come here?"

"You left me your phone number. I heard Daddy call you Mr. Keller. I went through all the Kellers in the book until I found the number you gave me, and there was the address."

Daniel gave the little boy's shoulder a friendly punch. "Good man. We could do with a few like you in the police."

Tommy's eyes shone. "Are you a policeman?" he asked fervently.

Daniel grimaced. "I used to think I was, but I'm afraid I'm not much of a policeman. Does anyone know you've gone?" Tommy shook his head. "Well, with any luck, you'll have time to see your mother and get back before they miss you."

Tommy looked at Daniel. "I'm not going back," he said quickly. "Never, ever. I've run away. I'm going to live with Mommy."

Daniel stared at him, gripped by dismay. Somehow this possibility had never occurred to him, and it opened up nightmare visions. To Tommy it was all so simple, but for Megan to keep him and Daniel to help her would get them both into deep trouble with the law, and that could be the final nail in the coffin of their hopes. "I expect you're hungry," he prevaricated. "I always was at your age." He started getting food out. "How did you escape?"

"Daddy's fiancée has moved in. She sent me to my room. She was cross because she says I make too much mess."

"Boys and mess just naturally go together," Daniel said, emptying a can of baked beans into a saucepan. "Doesn't she understand that?"

Tommy shook his head, his eyes on the food. "I was painting a picture and some of the paint got onto her dress. She said it was new." He added with nine-year-old masculine scorn, "She's always having new dresses."

Daniel nodded. "She looked the type."

"She wants me to go away to boarding school, but I want to be with Mommy." Suddenly his eyes filled with tears. "I want Mommy."

"And she wants you," Daniel said quickly. "Not just for today, but for the rest of your lives. We just have to find a way."

"I thought you'd have found it by now," Tommy said reproachfully. "When she came to see me at school that day—it *was* her, wasn't it?"

"Yes. I told her where you were, and she insisted on going there to see you. She'd have talked to you if she could, but we couldn't get any closer."

He set baked beans on toast in front of Tommy, who fell on them. "Are you having something to eat?" he asked, regarding Daniel with kindly concern.

"Thanks, but I don't have any appetite," Daniel responded with perfect truth. A pit was yawning at his feet. If only Megan would arrive soon.

At last, to his infinite relief, a car drew up outside, they both heard the door slam and the sound of running feet. Followed by Tommy, Daniel moved quickly into the hall. He opened the front door and stood back to let Megan see Tommy. She didn't even look at Daniel as she rushed inside and dropped to her knee to enfold her son in a hug. Tommy threw himself into her arms, hugging her tightly and burying his face against her. Daniel could hear a muffled cry of "Mommy, Mommy!"

From Megan there came no sound at all. Every fiber of her being was concentrated on holding her son tightly against her. Daniel hastily closed the front door, shielding them from the world, and watched her, trying to understand the pain in his heart. He knew that he no longer existed. He'd been a means to an end, and now that she'd achieved that end his usefulness was over. It hurt badly.

At last Megan pulled back and gazed eagerly into Tommy's face. Her own cheeks were stained with the tears that still ran down them, but her eyes were shining with joy. "Tommy, Tommy. Oh, my darling, you've changed—no you haven't . . . well, just a bit. You're still my Tommy. Oh, darling, darling." She was hugging and kissing him as she spoke, the words muffled by embraces. Tommy didn't say a word, just held on to his mother in a way that told its own story of yearning and loss.

Daniel looked away. *He* had caused this, and he couldn't bear it. And something else was hurting him: the memory of a boy's hug, arms tight around his neck, a whisper of "I love you, Daddy" from a child who knew the words would never be said in return. But it hadn't mattered. Neil had known he was loved, and he'd had the instinctive wisdom to realize that it was the knowledge that counted, not the words. Pictures flickered in Daniel's head: himself and Neil fishing, conspiring to buy Mommy's Christmas present that last year they were making up terrible puns together and laughing themselves silly. He'd spent time with Neil and had nothing to reproach himself for.

And yet . . . and yet . . . Now that it was too late, now that his son couldn't hear the words, he wished he'd managed to speak them. Just once. The sight of the two rapturous figures in each other's arms was more than he could bear to watch.

"I've missed you so much," Megan was saying. "All the time we were apart I longed for you."

"Daddy said you'd gone away forever," Tommy said, clinging to her. "He said you didn't love me anymore."

"That wasn't true," Megan said fiercely. "I love you more than anybody in the world, and I always will."

Daniel didn't catch Tommy's next words because he'd put his arms around his mother's neck again. He was full of apprehension. The thought of what Megan was going to say to him next filled him with dread, and he was right to be afraid. "Daniel, we've got to move fast," she said, rising but still holding on to Tommy with one hand. "They could be after us at any moment."

"Megan, exactly what are you planning to do?"

"Do? I'm going to keep Tommy with me, of course. We're going away together—"

"Where?"

"Where? What does it matter as long as we're together?"

"But how long will you be together? Your husband has legal custody. Technically what you're planning is kidnapping. You'll be on the run from the law, and they'll catch you and send him back." He knew the words were brutal, but he couldn't help it. He didn't know how much time he had to get through to her. He could see in her eyes that she was resisting the implication.

"I won't let them take him back," she insisted. "We'll go somewhere where nobody can find us."

"Megan, there isn't anywhere like that. They'll find you, and you'll be in a worse position than before."

"What are you saying?" she demanded wildly.

"I'm saying that I want you and Tommy to be together, too, but it has to be forever, and it won't be if you put yourself on the wrong side of the law now."

"Daniel—"

"If you want Tommy in the long run, he has to return to Brian tonight."

"*No!*" she screamed.

He took hold of her shoulders. "Listen to me, it's the only way."

"But I've only just got him back," she pleaded.

"And you'll get him back again, I promise, but next time it'll be for good."

He never knew how the conversation might have gone then if they hadn't been interrupted from an unexpected quarter. Tommy tugged gently at his mother, and said, "He's right, Mommy."

"*What?*" Megan dropped down to face the little boy again. "Tommy, darling, you don't mean that."

"Mr. Keller's right," Tommy repeated. "I have to go back so that we can be together again one day." He looked up at Daniel. "I guess I should be going now, sir," he said in an oddly mature voice. He turned to Megan. "Don't cry, Mommy. I'll come back."

His wisdom calmed Megan down. It was all true, she knew that. But the thought of saying goodbye to her child after such a brief reconciliation tore her apart. Tears sprang to her eyes but she fought them back. If Tommy was brave enough to do this without complaining, then she must match him for courage.

"There's something we must do first," Daniel replied. He picked up the telephone and dialed Brian's number. "Anderson," he said curtly when the phone was answered, "this is to let you know that your son's on his way home. He wanted to visit his mother, and now that he's done so, Megan is returning him. She's remained strictly within the law, so don't try to get clever." He put the phone down.

"You didn't have to do that," Megan said, incensed. "I wouldn't have gone back on my word."

"I was protecting you in case Anderson starts yelling 'kidnap,'" Daniel told her. "Let's go now."

Megan and Tommy spent the journey sitting together in the back of the car. There was so much she wanted to say to bridge the long gap, but there was too little time. She gave him the phone number of the boarding house, but she guessed Brian would be watching him like a hawk to prevent such a call.

Daniel spoke over his shoulder. "Tommy was telling me how he upset Selena Bracewell by getting paint over her things," he said.

"Darling, don't annoy her," Megan said quickly. "I don't want her to be unkind to you."

"She isn't," Tommy reassured her. "She just squeals and bursts into tears."

"I had an aunt like that," Daniel remembered. "I was a horrible child. I used to enjoy making her squeal by putting tadpoles in her shoes."

They'd stopped at a set of red lights. Daniel glanced over his shoulder long enough to wink at Tommy, who winked back. Megan missed this byplay. The mention of tadpoles had made her shudder. "Don't do anything like that, darling," she pleaded. "There's no knowing what that woman would do."

Daniel groaned. He could almost have sworn he heard Tommy groan, too. Although they couldn't see each other's faces, the atmosphere in the car was unmistakable. There were some things women just didn't understand.

All too soon they'd reached Brian's house. Megan glanced out of the window at what had once been her home, and flinched at the sight of Brian standing on the step. "Are you sure you're all right?" she asked Tommy anxiously, and he nodded.

Daniel stayed in the car as they both got out and walked to the front door, heads high. Brian looked at Tommy disapprovingly, but all he said was, "So you're home at last. Go into the kitchen, and Granny will give you something to eat."

Tommy squeezed Megan's hand once more, and stood on tiptoe to kiss her, ignoring his father's scowl, then he slipped away. Megan confronted her husband. "That was a very pretty little farce your friend the policeman played out for my benefit," Brian said coolly. "Visit, my foot! You'd have run away with him if Keller had let you."

"I've brought him back," she said, refusing to be provoked. "And now I've done that, I expect to be allowed to see him again."

"Not a chance. The next time Keller may not be around with his good sense and instinct for self-preservation."

Despite her good resolutions, she was jerked out of her composure. "What do you mean?"

"Oh, come on, Megan. Wise up. Why do you think he made you return Tommy? He's got his career to think of, hasn't he? He wants to get back into the force. He's not going to do that by helping you evade the law."

She managed to say, "Trust you to search for the worst in everyone."

"It's seldom necessary to search very far. I can see through a man like Keller better than you can. I knew what he wanted from you the day he came here. I've seen enough men slaver over you to know the look."

"You encouraged men to slaver over me when it suited you," she snapped.

He acknowledged this with a shrug. "Well, you encouraged Keller when it suited you. I don't blame you. It was common sense. But if you don't mind my giving you a little belated advice, you should have held out a little longer. He's had what he wanted by now, hasn't he? So why should he put his neck in the noose for you? I expect he told you returning Tommy was the best way to get him back in the long run, when your name's cleared. But just how close is he to clearing it? Not very close, is my guess. You should have kept him on the hook until he'd fulfilled his side of the bargain. It's too late now. Goodbye. Don't call again."

Before she could stop him, he shut the door in her face. Megan stood staring at it, feeling her body turn to ice. It couldn't be true. Daniel could never be as calculating and cynical as Brian suggested. That was just Brian's evil mind seeing everyone in his own light. But his accurate assessment of how Daniel had persuaded her touched a nerve.

Slowly she returned to the car and got in beside him. "Shall we go for a drink?" he asked.

"No, just take me back to the boarding house," she said quietly.

Daniel gave her a sharp glance, alerted by her tone, but he didn't say anything. Throughout the journey Megan sat in terrible brooding silence. She'd been a fool. Tommy had been there in her arms, and she'd given him back. Suddenly the ache of deprivation was with her again, a thousand times worse than it had ever been, and she had to bite her lip to stop herself from crying out a reproach.

When they reached the house, she said good-night quickly and got out of the car, plainly not wanting to see any more of him that night.

But Daniel followed her inside. "I have to talk to you," he said firmly. Ignoring her look of displeasure, he followed her up the stairs and into her room.

As soon as the door was closed, she turned and confronted him. Her face was calm but pale, and closed against him. "Please, Daniel, there's nothing to say. I know that . . . technically . . . you were right. Let's leave it at that."

"But you're not leaving it at that, are you? In your heart you still condemn me."

"All right," she flashed. "There are some things that might be technically right—and wise, and clever, and sensible—but a man with an ounce of feeling still couldn't bring himself to do them."

"A man with an ounce of feeling wouldn't let you run off with Tommy and get yourself into the kind of trouble that would mean you might never see him again," he said deliberately.

"He's my son," she cried passionately. "It's as though he's been dead, and I got him back. I held him in my arms flesh and blood. He was real—not a dream or a shadow, but real—and you took him away. . . ." Her grief made the words pour out almost incoherently.

As always, her pain devastated him. He reached out and took hold of her. "I want to get him back for you, but that's not the way," he said, trying to soothe her.

"It's not the legal way, and the legal way is the only way that counts—isn't it?—you . . . you *policeman*."

He ignored the insult and pulled her close, trying to kiss her face, her tears, but she twisted away from him, pushing him back so hard that he staggered and lost his balance, almost falling to the floor. "Don't touch me," she said hoarsely. "You were right, and I was wrong. There, I've admitted it, so everything's nice and tidy for you, isn't it? You've stopped me from breaking the law, and you've saved yourself from being implicated, and they'll remember that when they come to let you back into the force."

She hadn't meant to say those last cruel words, and she was shocked at herself when she saw the effect they had on him. His face actually went gray. "Is that what you think, Megan?" he asked quietly.

"I don't know, Daniel. You tell me what to think."

He shook his head. "That's just what I can't do."

Without another word, he turned and went out.

Eleven

Megan listened to Daniel's footsteps going down the stairs. She knew she should run after him and apologize, but her limbs seemed to have turned to ice. Her legs gave way, and she sat down suddenly on the bed, burying her face in her hands, wondering how she could have been so wicked as to hurt him. She'd repeated Brian's malicious accusation mindlessly, as though her ex-husband was a man to be respected, when she knew better. She'd accused Daniel of being heartless, forgetting that his own son was dead, and he understood her feelings better than anyone.

At last she moved her hands away, and realized that she was staring at Daniel's wallet lying on the floor. It must have dropped out when he nearly fell, and neither of them had noticed. Swiftly Megan snatched up the wallet and hurried out in pursuit, but she was only just in time to see his taillights vanishing into the dis-

tance. She looked frantically up and down the street.
As if in answer to a prayer, Bert's cab pulled up to the
curb. He started to get out, yawning. "End of another
shift, thank goodness," he said.

"Bert, I need your help," she pleaded.

"Have I got to get back into that car?" he asked.

"Please. My friend's gone off without his wallet. I
have to catch him."

"All right. Get in."

She got in beside him and said urgently, "You can
just see him in the distance."

Bert started up and managed to get a little nearer to
Daniel's car, but without warning they found themselves in heavy traffic and it was impossible to get really close. "Football match," he said laconically. "The
crowd's just come out."

"Can't you catch up a bit more?" Megan pleaded.

"It's as much as I can do to keep him in sight."

Suddenly Megan gave a little gasp of relief. "What's
the matter with me? I'm panicking for nothing. I know
where he lives. We can just go straight to his house. We
might even get there first." She gave Bert the address.

"Are you sure?" Bert asked, frowning.

"Of course I'm sure."

"Well, he's taking a funny way home, then. He's just
turned left at the traffic light. If he was going where
you said, he'd have gone right."

"But I know I've got the correct address."

"Perhaps he's not going home, then?"

"At this time of night? He must be."

Bert cleared his throat awkwardly. "There isn't another lady in the picture, by any chance?"

"No, there isn't," she said crisply.

"All right, I only asked."

But as the journey continued, it became clear to Megan that Daniel wasn't going home. He was going somewhere else that he'd never told her about. A faint frisson of unease went through her. Of course she had no right to know every detail of Daniel's life. It was just...

It was just that he'd seemed so completely absorbed in her and her problems, as though the two of them existed in a world apart, that it came as an unpleasant shock to discover that this was an illusion. That was all it was, of course. She'd simply lost her sense of proportion. It was none of her business where Daniel was going. "Step on the gas," she said tersely. "Don't lose him, whatever you do."

For the next fifteen minutes they wove in and out of traffic in a way that put all Bert's skills to the test. At last, to their relief, they saw Daniel turn in through a pair of iron gates. A car cut across, forcing them to delay until he was out of sight, but when they were able to follow, they found a long drive leading to a large house. Daniel's car was parked at the bottom of a flight of broad steps, but he was nowhere to be seen.

"Shall I wait?" Bert asked. "Or will he bring you home?"

"I'll manage, thanks, Bert. Go home to bed. How much do I owe you?"

She began to take out her purse, but he growled "Get out of here" and quickly drove off.

She ran up the stairs and through a set of double doors, coming to a halt in a hallway. "Can I help you?" asked a young woman behind a desk.

"Can you tell me what this place is?" Megan asked, bewildered. She'd rushed in too fast to take much notice of details, but now she realized that this wasn't a private house but some sort of official building.

"This is Netherham Hospital," said the young woman.

"A hospital?"

"How did you get here if you didn't know that?"

"I followed Mr. Keller. He left his wallet behind."

"Oh, he's just down that corridor with his son."

Megan stared. "His son? But I thought his son was dead."

The receptionist sighed. "Well, he might as well be. The injuries he sustained in the accident healed long ago, but he's never awakened."

"He's been in a coma for three years?" Megan asked, thunderstruck. She repeated to herself, *Three years*. She pulled herself together. "How often does he come here?"

"Several times a week," the receptionist said sympathetically. "There's no set pattern, because of his job. Although..." She lowered her voice. "Although I understand he's lost his job, so he might have to take Neil away, poor man."

"I beg your pardon?"

"Well, the fees of this place are sky-high. I don't know how he's managed them. Look, I shouldn't be gossiping about him like this—"

"Go on," Megan said urgently. "There are things I need to know."

"Well, between you and me, he's sometimes been a bit late with the payments, but he's always managed it in the end. But now...well, all that trouble, being thrown off the force—you know..."

Megan moved aside out of the light, but it was clear the receptionist hadn't recognized her. "I'd heard something," she agreed cautiously.

"Wasn't that a terrible thing to happen to him? Everyone here loves that little boy so much, and if he has to take him away—well, it doesn't bear thinking about. Sometimes he stays at Neil's bedside all night. It must be heartbreaking for him. The child doesn't know he's there, but he never gives up hope."

Megan could hardly speak. "Which room did you say?"

"Just down there. Number 15. But look, I'm not sure I should let you—"

"It's all right," Megan said. "I'm his friend. At least, I thought I was."

She made her way cautiously down the corridor until she came to Number 15 and peered through the window in the door. At first she could see little, for the room was only dimly lit. Then she made out the bed with the small form lying on it, the dark head motionless on the pillow. Beside the bed, his back to her, sat Daniel. He was hunched forward and even at this angle Megan could tell that his eyes were fixed on the child with a terrible anguish that blotted out everything else in the world.

Nobody knew that anguish better than herself, and tears started in Megan's eyes as she contemplated the hunched figure, sitting in lonely faithfulness by the child who was oblivious of him. She pressed closer to the glass, holding her breath. Then Daniel turned and saw her.

She was horrified at being discovered like this. For a moment he just stared at her, as if he couldn't believe the evidence of his own eyes. Megan quietly opened the door and stepped inside. "Megan, what are you doing here?" Daniel's voice was controlled, but he sounded uneasy.

"You left your wallet behind," she said quickly, "and I followed you with it. I didn't catch up until we reached here."

He took the wallet she handed him. "I see. Thank you."

"I wasn't prying, Daniel, truly. But you don't want me here, do you?"

He seemed to answer with an effort. "Why should you say that?"

"Because you didn't tell me your son was still alive. When we talked the other evening you let me think he'd died with your wife."

"I didn't do that on purpose, it's just..." He shrugged. "I find it hard to speak of him at all."

"And after the dreadful things I said to you to-night—"

"That doesn't matter. You were overwrought. I've forgotten it already."

But she could feel that he was still keeping her at arm's length, and suddenly it was terribly important that he allow her to come close. Summoning all her courage, Megan closed the door behind her and went over to the bed. A child lay there in complete stillness. His face looked as if it might once have held mischief, but sleep had wrapped him in a protective blanket, keeping him apart from the world. "He's been like that for three years," Daniel said bleakly.

"He looks as if he's only just dozed off," Megan said.

"I know. That's the hardest part. It doesn't look like a coma at all. I keep expecting him to open his eyes and say 'Hello, Daddy.'" Daniel's voice grew husky on the last words.

"I wish you'd told me about him," Megan said. "I might have been more understanding. I've thought of little except my own troubles."

"You've had plenty of those. You were entitled to think of them."

"But not entitled to forget that other people have troubles, too," Megan said.

"Perhaps he's part of the damage I've done," Daniel said somberly. "In those first weeks after the accident I should have spent more time with him, talking to him, trying to call him back to life. If I'd done that, instead of trying to prove how on top of everything I was, I might have spared you a tragedy, and he— Well, who knows what might have happened?"

"Daniel, don't torment yourself with ifs. You think if you'd talked to him then he might have come round, but he probably wouldn't. If he's been asleep this long it's because he needed to be." She had no idea whether this was true or not, but she was saying anything that might help him.

"Perhaps. I don't know. I only know that I've become... well, superstitious is the word, I suppose."

"How do you mean?"

"My arrogance and stupidity in working when I wasn't capable lost you your son. Perhaps it lost me mine, too. I should have been here. And I can't get it out of my head that if only I can restore Tommy to you, then maybe... maybe—" He couldn't finish but his eyes were on the terribly still child, and his hand groped for Megan's. She twined her fingers in his and held him tightly. "Just silly superstition," he said after a moment. "I know you think what I made you do tonight was very hard, but I didn't have an ulterior motive, Megan, I swear I didn't. Anderson would have moved heaven and earth to have you put back in jail.''

"I know," she whispered. "Tommy saw it before I did. He trusted you at once."

"Tommy and I are going to get on well." Daniel gave a sigh. "If only I could find the way through to Neil."

"Don't you talk to him now?"

Daniel hesitated. "I sit with him," he said at last, "but I don't talk much. I don't know what to say anymore."

"What about the things you shared? If he can hear you, he'd surely like to remember those?"

"But they were all so long ago."

"I don't think that matters. If memories are all you have, then you should make the most of them. Didn't you use to do things together?"

"Yes, plenty."

"Fishing, and such like?"

"Yes, we did that. And mechanical things, too. He was very mechanically minded—"

"*Is* mechanically minded," Megan corrected him gently. "You should never say was. He's only asleep, Daniel. And someday he's going to awaken."

"Is he? Or am I deluding myself with false hopes?"

"I used to think that, but my false hopes became true hopes. It *can* happen. But you have to believe in it."

"But how do I go on believing in the face of nothing? No response at all, nothing."

She gave him a sad little smile. "The same way that I went on believing in the face of gray walls."

He searched her face as she said this, and he saw no trace of the bitterness that had once been in her eyes when she spoke of her prison sentence. It was gone now, replaced by a gentle sympathy. She'd called up her own tragedy not to reproach him but to give him hope, and it was this, more than her words, that acted on his spirit, reviving his courage.

"Talk to me about Neil," she said. "Tell me about how mechanical he is."

Daniel began, stumbling a little until he got the hang of it. "He could always mend things better than I could—plugs and stuff. You've seen the room with the audio-video equipment. That was—*is*—our room. When we'd read instructions he always understood them before I did and explained them to me sometimes. And he was only seven."

"That's incredible," she said encouragingly.

"He used to laugh at me because I was so slow—but kindly. He was—*is*—a very kind boy."

"What's he like with a computer?" Megan asked.

"A wizard. You should see him, Megan."

"Ah, but can he program a video recorder?" she asked, suddenly inspired.

To her delight, Daniel caught the ball she'd tossed and ran with it. "Can he...? Can he program a video recorder? I tell you, the video isn't made that can defeat this boy."

Megan took a calculated gamble. Turning to Neil, she spoke directly. "Then you'd better awaken soon and show the rest of us," she said, risking a touch of comedy. "I know you can hear me. Think of all the things you're missing. They're bringing out new machines every day. You could be using them."

"On the day you come out I'll buy you the best computer in the business." Daniel took up the theme.

"We'll learn it together. We always did things together, didn't we? And we'll do them again."

Neil lay without moving. Not by so much as a flicker did he show any response. Daniel's shoulders sagged. "He can't hear me," he said wearily. "I'm just fooling myself."

"Then fool yourself," Megan said urgently. "Fool yourself as I did during those years I was telling myself I was bound to be set free eventually. Fool yourself, and go on fooling yourself if it's the only way to hang on to your belief. Sometimes only the fools are wise."

Then Daniel did something that brought an ache to Megan's throat. He looked down on the still, pale figure on the bed and held out his hand. "Put it there," he said. And he himself lifted the lifeless little hand to hold in his great fist. "That was what we used to do," he explained to Megan. "It was our way of saying we were close...that we understood each other...that we l—" His voice trailed away.

"I'll wait for you outside," Megan said, and quietly left the room.

Left alone with his son, Daniel placed his other hand over the little boy's, enclosing it between both his. "She's nice, isn't she?" he asked awkwardly. "You're going to like her when...if—I don't know. There's so much has to happen first. So many mountains to climb. But we'll all get there." He searched Neil's face for a long time before saying softly, "I love you, son. You always knew that, really, didn't you? Even if I didn't say it."

After waiting a long time in vain, he leaned down and kissed the child. Then he left the room.

When they were sitting in the car, Megan said, "Daniel, please take me back to your home."

He didn't look at her. "Are you sure?"

"Quite sure. I've been blinkered and self-absorbed, but I see a lot of things clearly now." She touched his arm. "Please."

He drove her home without another word.

That night their lovemaking was gentle, fervent but not fierce. The tigress sheathed her claws and touched her lover languidly in silky caresses. Her eyes gleamed at him in the night, but their glow was soft and full of love. She was still a creature of the jungle, but she'd chosen to be tame—just for tonight. Tomorrow it would be different, but now her growl was a purr and her danger was hidden.

When they'd taken their fill of each other and lay in each other's arms, Daniel said hesitantly, "I'm not wrong, am I, Megan? What I think has happened to us...has really happened?"

"Yes," she murmured contentedly against his chest. "It's really happened. I've been trying to believe it, too."

"How did you and I come to fall in love?" he marveled. "The two least likely people in the world."

"Perhaps we're not so unlikely, after all," she mused. "We two know things that nobody else knows. Who else can understand either of us as well as we understand each other?"

A gleam of humor lit his habitually stern face as he said, "And do you think that's the basis of what's between us—understanding? Companionship? Respect and esteem? Admiration for each other's intelligence?"

She smiled. "Well, I think we have those, too. But it's not the whole story."

"No, it certainly isn't," he said, tightening his hold on her. "None of them mean a damn thing without this...." He kissed her purposefully and she felt the magic begin again, "And this," he added, turning his body so that she lay beneath him and he could gaze down at her.

He'd meant to look his fill, but after only a moment her beauty was too much for him and he began to love her again. She received him joyfully, feeling not only love but an overwhelming relief that they'd found a way to confess the truth to each other, and now there need be no further barriers. He was her man because he needed as well as loved her, and he could see into her heart as nobody else in the world could do.

When at last Daniel lay asleep, Megan raised herself up on one elbow and looked down at him with eyes that were tender.

"It's gone on long enough," she whispered. "I want everything. I want you, and I want my son back, and I won't wait any longer. You're a policeman. You have to do it by the book. But let's face it—doing it by the book isn't working."

She regarded him again for a moment before murmuring thoughtfully, "But *I'm* not a policeman."

Twelve

For a moment Jackson Grainger seemed to have difficulty in focusing his eyes as he peered into the gloom of the hallway outside his door. "Who are you?" he demanded of the woman standing there.

"Surely you remember me, Mr. Grainger? Three years isn't all that long, and there are, shall we say, good reasons for me to lodge in your memory."

"Good grief! I heard they'd let you out, but I didn't think you'd dare show your face around here again. Hey, I didn't invite you in."

"But I seem to be in now, don't I? I'm surprised you weren't expecting me. We have so much to talk about."

"I've got nothing to talk about with the woman who murdered my uncle," Grainger said loftily.

"Come now, that's very ungrateful, surely?" Megan had managed to get well into the apartment, the very apartment where Henry Grainger had died, and which was now occupied by his nephew. She dropped onto the sofa in such a position that her short skirt rode up, giving Jackson Grainger a grandstand view of her incredibly long silken legs. She smiled up at him knowingly.

"I don't know what you mean by ungrateful," he said uneasily.

"Well, look at you now—set up in comfort, the owner of this apartment block. At the time your uncle died your circumstances were very, very different. You were deep in debt and had some nasty characters on your trail. Let's face it, whoever killed Uncle Henry did you a big favor."

An expression of self-conscious virtue settled over the man's pasty face. "I think that remark's in very poor taste."

Megan's beautifully arched eyebrows rose. "Really? I think it's spot on."

"I'd like you to leave."

"I'm sure you would. I'm sure the mere sight of me makes you uneasy—almost as uneasy as the fact that I was cleared. The police will be asking questions again now. That prospect must be giving you a few nasty moments."

"Don't you try to frighten me," Grainger blustered.

"I wouldn't dream of it. You're quite scared enough without any help from me. Why don't you offer me a drink?" She smiled temptingly. "I can remember when you used to keep asking me to have a drink with you."

"Yes, and you were always too high and mighty," he said in an aggrieved voice. He went to the liquor cabinet. "Any preference?"

"Vodka, please."

Grainger poured himself a stiff whiskey and handed Megan her glass. He seemed to have recovered some of his poise. "You can talk all the nonsense you want," he said. "I don't mind having a drink with you. Not so high and mighty now, eh?"

"Let's say I'm ready to discuss things reasonably. You might find yourself in the same frame of mind."

"Don't kid yourself. I'm in the clear. I had an alibi for that night."

"Not a very good alibi," Megan mused. "It depended on a lady who expected to share your good fortune, and is rather put out at being dumped. My impression was that for two pins she'd tell a very different story."

For the first time, a shade of unease crept into the man's manner. "What do you mean, your impression? You haven't seen her. You can't fool me."

"Oh, I've seen her all right," Megan said, smiling in a way that brought him no comfort at all. "We had a very interesting talk."

Grainger gulped down some whiskey. "It's all lies," he asserted in a voice that just managed to keep steady.

"Well, if you don't know what she's saying about you, how do you know that they're lies?" Megan asked reasonably.

"Look here, what do you want?"

Megan sipped her vodka delicately. "I suppose I want justice. I went to jail for your crime, Mr. Grainger, while you've lived well off the proceeds. Now, that doesn't seem right to me. I have a fairly good idea how you did it. You came to see your uncle that night, and you arrived while he was upstairs with me. You heard us quarreling. The whole building heard us. You heard me say that he wasn't fit to live. You waited for him to come down and waylaid him at the door of his apartment. That's how come nobody heard you ring his bell.''

She stopped and glanced inquiringly at Grainger, who'd gone a ghastly color and was regarding her with horrible fascination. When he caught her looking at him directly, he swiftly avoided her gaze by returning to his drink. ''Perhaps you were already thinking of killing him,'' Megan mused in a judicious tone. ''And perhaps the decision was finally taken when you saw him come downstairs with my ashtray. With that and the quarrel, you knew you could point the finger at me. You killed him, knowing that you'd inherit, and you persuaded Mary Aylmer and her brother to give you an alibi. But once I'd been convicted, you dumped them.

''I suppose you thought you were safe enough. You paid her off with five hundred pounds every three months.'' To Megan's satisfaction this precise figure caused Grainger to blanch. ''Not very much, but more than she'd get if she exposed you. No, she wasn't likely to give you away, and even if she'd done so, who'd have believed her? Our legal system doesn't like admitting it's made a mistake, and once I'd been found guilty nobody would have *wanted* to believe her.''

Grainger was staring at her belligerently. ''So?'' he demanded.

''So...that was then. This is now. They've had to admit they were mistaken about me. That makes the police very annoyed. They need to save their faces by finding the real murderer. I reckon they'd give Mary a deal—no prosecution in return for evidence about you.'' To her immense satisfaction, she saw Grainger swallow. His face was a sickly hue.

But he recovered himself enough to say, "You're bluffing."

She shrugged. "As you wish. I just thought you might want to talk to me before you talk to the police. But if you're sure you can cope with them without my help...well, I'll be going."

"Wait. What do you mean, without your help? Why should you help me?"

"For the same reason that you should help me. Mutual interest, Mr. Grainger. I took the rap, you took the money. I could always take the heat off you—for a consideration."

"What...do you mean?"

"I've nothing to lose, have I? I've been released, I can't be sent back to jail. They can think me as guilty as they like, but I'll stay free. I could arrange for the evidence to point back to me...if I wanted to. At the moment, it points to you."

"And what's the price?"

"Money. A lot of it."

"You've got a nerve."

Instead of answering directly, Megan looked around her. "This is a beautiful place, and I must say you've done it up very nicely. It would be a pity if you weren't here to enjoy it."

"How much?"

"Twenty grand."

"That's more than I can raise."

"I don't think so. Your uncle used to boast to me about how rich he was. It depends on how much you prize your freedom. And make no mistake, Mr. Grainger, your freedom is under threat." Seeing him swallow again, Megan went on casually, "I don't think you'd like prison. Take it from someone who's been there, you wouldn't like it at all. Fancy your being so lucky all this time! Well, everyone's luck runs out sometime.''

"Who says my luck's run out?" Grainger asked slowly. "You mentioned a deal."

"That's right. We can be good to each other. After all, why shouldn't we share his money? We both suffered enough because of him. I hated him, and I know you did."

"Evil old scroat," Grainger concurred. "He knew I was desperate for money, and he could have helped me. But not him. He enjoyed taunting me with it, saying I'd come into it all after he'd gone, and just be a little patient. And all the time he was trying to find a way to break the settlement and cut me out."

"Perhaps he found it?" Megan suggested, inspired.

"According to him, he *had*. I dunno if it was true, or whether it was just him tormenting me, but he said it could be done with a bit of time."

"That was silly of him," Megan observed. "That was practically begging you to cut his time short. I'd say he got what he asked for."

Grainger gave a sudden crack of laughter. "You should have seen his face when he saw me lift that ashtray."

"I'll bet it was worth seeing." Megan chuckled.

"It would almost have been worth a jail sentence to get back at him," Grainger mused.

"But you didn't have to go to jail," she told him. "You were cleverer than that."

"I was cleverer than you think, Miss Smarty Boots. I didn't waylay him at the door of his apartment. I picked the lock and was waiting for him when he got in. Nobody ever knew I was there."

"Now that was *really* clever," Megan agreed.

Grainger came and sat down beside her. "So," he said, breathing whiskey fumes all over her, "me and you is going to do business. So how about we seal our pact properly?"

"What do you mean?"

"Let's start with a little kiss."

"I never mix business with pleasure," she said firmly.

"Well, I do. It's the best way. After all, we're gonna be tied together pretty close in future, and that'll suit me. Come on, stop acting like a prude."

He made a lunge toward her. Megan fended him off, but his weight bore her backward onto the sofa. She twisted her head away to stop his kissing her, but he began groping around her body with heavy hands. Then suddenly he grew still. *"What's this?"*

He thrust a hand inside her blouse, wrenched at something and brought his hand out clutching some wire. "You bitch!" he said furiously. "You're wired."

"And connected to a police van," she said breathlessly. "So be careful what you do."

Fury made his face livid. Megan stared up at him, realizing that this man had killed once and she was at his mercy. Far away, she heard shouts, the sounds of banging doors, but all her attention was for Jackson Grainger's hands, moving inexorably toward her neck, tightening around her throat. There was a terrifying moment when he seemed to be squeezing the life out of her, then he suddenly vanished. The weight crushing her disappeared, air rushed back into her lungs, and Daniel was pulling her up and cradling her in his arms.

"My God," he murmured. "I should never have let you take such a risk."

"It was the only way." She gasped. "Did you get it?"

"Every word, loud and clear."

He helped her to sit up. The room seemed to be filled with policemen. Two of them were restraining Grainger, who was shouting with fury. "Careful with him, Canvey," Daniel warned. "That's a very costly cargo you've got there."

"Don't you worry," a plump, amiable-looking man replied. "It's so costly that we're going to lock it up for safety. Jackson Grainger, I arrest you for the murder of your uncle, Henry Grainger. You are not obliged to say anything. . . ." He recited the rest of the warning.

"You bitch!" Grainger raged at Megan. "You wait. Just you wait—"

"It'll be a long wait," Canvey observed. "Get him out of here."

Still struggling, Grainger was hauled to the door. "Are you all right?" Canvey asked Megan, who was feeling her throat.

"I'm going to be all right now," she said, her eyes on Daniel.

"Right, then, I'll be off with my prisoner. I'll give Chief Inspector Masters your regards, Daniel, and tell him you'll be in to see him soon."

"Tell him anything you like," Daniel said, turning to Megan. Holding her close, he said, "I was so scared all the time you were in here. I should never have let you talk me into it."

"Daniel, let's get out of here. I hate this place."

"Right now," he agreed, taking her by the hand.

They ran from the building like a couple of children, hurrying to the car, and talking in excited bursts all the way home. They didn't make much sense, but they didn't care. They were too excited and happy.

Without asking her, Daniel headed for his own house. He wanted her with him tonight, and they would celebrate the way the future had been transformed for them both. There were still problems to be overcome, but right this minute anything seemed possible.

They shut the front door behind them, laughing and kissing. "I want a cup of tea," Megan said. "My throat feels rough after the treatment Grainger gave it."

There was a sheet of paper on the kitchen table that she glanced at idly. Then she stiffened. "Daniel, there's a message from Gladys. It looks urgent."

Daniel picked up the note the cleaning woman had written.

The hospital called at midday to say you should go there quickly. I tried calling your car phone but couldn't get through.

Watching Daniel, Megan saw his face go gray. "Oh, my God!" he whispered. He raised tortured eyes to her. "I didn't have it mended...she couldn't call me. *Neil*—" He sat down at the table in shock.

"We'll call now," Megan said urgently. "What's the number?"

But he stopped her, gripping her wrist hard. "No," he said. "Don't call, not just yet."

"But Daniel, it must be about Neil."

"I know that," he said hoarsely. "That's why. Don't you see? It's been twelve hours since they called."

"Perhaps they want to tell you that he's improved."

He gave her a desperate look. "Perhaps. Perhaps after three years there's been a miracle—only I don't believe in miracles."

"But I do," she said quickly. "I know they happen, because only a miracle can explain the way you came back into my life to rescue me. Just a little time ago everything was black, but then there was a miracle. If I can have one, you can, too."

"I wish I could believe that, but I can't. I should call them but . . . Megan . . ." He searched her face, seeking the courage to make the terrible admission. *"I'm afraid."*

She reached out and took him into her arms, holding him close, vainly seeking the words that could protect him from the possibility of his son's death. But there were none. The only comfort she could offer was the warmth of her presence and the power of her love. Now that he'd brought himself to make the admission of vulnerability he'd always resisted, her love flowed more freely than ever. She wanted to surround him with love, and keep him safe forever, but there was so little she could do.

"Don't call yet," he begged. "If he's dead, I don't want to know. Let me hope for a little while longer." He tightened his arms suddenly, burying his face against her. "I can't face it," he cried in agony.

"You can, my dearest," she murmured, "if you have to. But it may be good news."

"Not after all this time. Hold me, Megan. Without you I have no courage. Don't let me go."

She gave up trying to talk and did as he asked. Once she'd been the weak one, but thanks to Daniel she'd recovered her strength and part of her life. He'd given her something else, too, something whose wonder she was rediscovering every day. Now she strained every fiber of her being to return the gift.

"Do you want me to call the hospital?" she asked softly. He shook his head, his face still buried against her. "All right, we'll just go there."

For a moment he didn't move, and she thought he might really refuse, but at last he seemed to become conscious of her urging him to his feet, and got up. She led him out of the house toward the car. When he'd produced the key and opened the door, he said bleakly, "I'm afraid you'll have to drive."

Through a thousand emergencies, in life-and-death situations, his nerve had never failed. But now suddenly he felt as if he'd been turned to jelly. He could only be thankful that this strong woman was there to protect him. When he learned the worst, she, who'd endured so much, would be at his side to teach him how to endure.

They made the journey in silence. When they reached the hospital, Daniel was slumped in his seat. "Daniel," she said gently. When he didn't respond, she leaned over and kissed him.

"It's all right," he said. "I can cope now, as long as you're with me."

Together they walked into the hospital. The receptionist looked up quickly. "Mr. Keller, thank goodness you're here. Dr. Walker would like to talk to you before you see Neil."

"Is that necessary?" he asked quietly. "I mean, does it really matter why it happened? I suppose, in my heart, I always knew it was inevitable."

"Yes, you always had faith, didn't you?" the receptionist said, smiling. "We're all so happy for you."

For a moment Daniel simply didn't take it in. He just stared at her while her meaningless words reverberated around his head. It was Megan who understood and began to weep with joy. "Daniel, don't you see?" she said, shaking him slightly. "Neil isn't dead. He's awakened."

"What?" He stared at her before turning quickly back to the receptionist. "Was that what you meant? Is that it? *Is that it?*"

"But of course. Good heavens, whatever were you thinking?"

Daniel didn't answer. Following blind instinct, he turned to Megan and they threw themselves into each other's arms. For a long moment they stood there, seemingly motionless, but actually Megan could feel his shoulders shaking with sobs. She didn't speak, but stroked his hair and tried to communicate her joy silently.

A doctor appeared and started wringing his hands. "This is a great day," he said. "Everyone here is delighted for you. Neil simply opened his eyes a few hours ago. Why don't you go along and see him now?"

Dazed, Daniel made his way down the corridor to his son's room, with Megan following. A smiling nurse rose from the bedside and stepped back to let him come close. "He's dropped off to sleep again," she said.

Daniel sat down beside the motionless child, looking searchingly into his face. Neil looked the same as he had done a few days ago, and Megan knew a sudden fear lest he'd slipped back into the coma. The doctor and nurse went quietly out and closed the door. Megan wondered if she, too, should go and leave father and son together, but then she saw that Daniel was so absorbed in his child that it didn't matter if she went or stayed. He was talking to Neil, and although the words were softly spoken, she could hear every one in the quiet room.

"You awoke, and I wasn't here for you. After three years, I failed you. What did you think when you opened your eyes and found me not there? Did you decide to go away again? Don't do that to me... please—"

Megan watched the child's face in an agony of apprehension. Inwardly she was praying, *Don't do this to him. He's suffered so much. Don't ask him to bear any more.*

But it seemed that the time for Daniel's miracle hadn't come, for the silence went on and on, and Megan saw the death of hope in his sagging shoulders and lowered head. "I guess that's it," he said heavily. "It was a false dawn."

"Daniel, please don't... Daniel, *look.*"

But he'd seen it, too, the moment when Neil's eyelids fluttered. They both held their breaths, and gradually the child's eyes opened slowly, leaving him looking directly at his father. "Hello, Daddy," he murmured.

Daniel reached out his hand. He meant to say "Put it there," as he'd always done, but no words would come, and suddenly he couldn't see for the tears that poured down his face. He dropped his head on his arm, and after a moment he felt his hand squeezed by a small childish one.

Megan slipped noiselessly out the door.

It was an hour before he joined her. His face was glowing. "He talked to me," he said. "He's going to be all right. You didn't need to go."

"It's best that I did," she said. "I've just realized so many things. For you, Sally has been dead for three years. But for him it's only just happened."

Daniel shook his head. "He knows," he said. "He told me before I could tell him. In a strange way he's known all the time. It's as though she's been with him these three years, and they've said their goodbyes peacefully. He'll be ready when I introduce him to…his new mother?" He looked at her inquiringly and she nodded, her heart too full for speech.

On the journey back to Daniel's house Megan was torn between joy and sadness. With all her heart she rejoiced for Daniel, but still there was an ache when she thought of Tommy. Daniel's happiness in his son's recovery only underlined the separation from her own son. "Daniel," she ventured, "now that everything else is settled, Tommy…"

"We're going to get him back," he promised. "We'll go to court and— Hello, what's that?"

As they turned the corner of his street they saw a large, ostentatious car parked outside Daniel's house. It had plainly been chosen for its appearance, just as the woman standing beside it had the look of a creature to whom appearance was everything. She was peering crossly up and down the street, drumming on the car roof with long, painted nails, and occasionally patting her elaborately coiffed blond hair. She stood up straight when Daniel's car pulled up to the curb.

"You took your time getting here," she said crossly, as though they should have been expecting her.

"Who are you?" Megan asked.

"Selena Bracewell," Daniel said, recognizing the woman in the photograph on Brian Anderson's desk.

"It's a pleasure to meet you at last, Miss Bracewell. I hope I'm not too late to congratulate you on your approaching nuptials."

Megan stared at him. *"Daniel!"* she protested. To her astonishment his eyes were sparkling with some emotion she didn't understand.

Daniel could hardly contain his excitement. What Megan had seen in his eyes was triumph as he sensed a winner about to cross the finish line with flags flying. But he didn't have time to explain.

Receiving no answer from him, Megan turned her attention back to Selena Bracewell. "Has something happened to Tommy?" she asked.

"Nothing's happened to Tommy—yet," Selena said with bitter emphasis. "But something's going to happen if he doesn't get out of my hair, out of my car, and out of my life. Come on, you. Get moving." She addressed the last words to someone inside her car who was already scrambling out. The next moment Megan gave a cry of joy as Tommy rushed into her arms.

Selena began hauling bags from the backseat, and dumping them into the road. "These are his things," she said. "Just get him out of my sight. I told his father he could choose between me and that brat from hell, and Brian said I could do whatever I liked. So I'm doing it."

"What, er, precipitated this?" Daniel inquired with deceptive innocence.

"Tadpoles," Selena Bracewell said bitterly. "Tadpoles everywhere. Even in my shoes. And some of them were more than tadpoles. *A frog jumped out at me.* It's not what I'm used to, and I'm not going to start getting used to it."

"You won't have to," Daniel assured her kindly. "Please don't worry, Miss Bracewell. We'll take full charge of this dangerous delinquent, and you'll never be troubled with him again." He glanced at Megan and Tommy, still embracing, and added in an undertone, "If Anderson tries to change his mind, tell him it's too late."

"If he dares to change his mind I'll tell him a sight more than that." Selena seethed. "Don't you worry. Leave Brian to me."

"I'm sure we can," Daniel remarked smoothly. Selena gave him a dark look, got back into her car and sped away. "Let's get inside," Daniel said to the other two.

They closed the door on the outside world, shutting themselves in with their happiness. Tommy grinned at Daniel, who held out his hand. "Put it there," he said, and Tommy did so.

"I don't understand," Megan said, looking at the two of them.

"You don't have to," Daniel told her. He grinned back at Tommy. "We understand, don't we?" Tommy nodded. "You don't think an actual frog was overdoing it a bit?"

"Oh, no," Tommy said instantly. "You see, I knew I wouldn't get another chance, and I wanted to be quite sure."

"Quite right," Daniel agreed.

"Will somebody tell me what's going on?" Megan demanded.

As one, the other two shook their heads. "Leave it, Megan," Daniel advised. "This is man talk. Why don't you two go into the next room and catch up on lost time, while I get us something to eat?"

He did more than that. With perfect tact, he made himself scarce for the next few hours, leaving mother and son together. Megan and Tommy spent only a small part of that time talking. The rest was spent just sitting together on the sofa, wrapped in each other's arms. There would be time enough for talking in the days to come.

When Tommy could no longer control his yawns, she led him upstairs to the bedroom that Daniel had readied for him. She stayed with him until he fell asleep, then tiptoed out to where Daniel was waiting for her.

"You're a saint," she whispered, "to be so patient."

He lifted her up in his arms and carried her along the hallway, kicking open the door of his room. "But I'm not going to be patient any longer," he said.

Much later that night as they lay drowsily in each other's arms, Megan murmured, "I'm going to be really outnumbered by men in this household. You, Neil, Tommy..."

"Well you know the remedy for that, don't you?" he muttered, beginning to kiss her again.

"Tell me."

"We should set about having a daughter as soon as possible," he said, drawing her into his arms. "Say, in about nine months?"

It was he who slept first, resting with his head on her breast. Megan held him there protectively, thinking about this man that she loved with all her heart and soul, thinking about the son who'd come back to her, and about Daniel's son, soon to come home, who would need so much care.

A daughter would be a great blessing, but she already had so many blessings that would once have seemed impossible. How could she possibly ask for more?

But then she looked down at the man who lay so trustingly against her, and she realized that it was pointless to worry, and futile to make plans. Blessings were given, not earned, and whoever it was that allocated them would give this one, too, when the time was right. Meanwhile, she had only to wait, and love.

* * * * *

Take 4 bestselling love stories FREE

Plus get a FREE surprise gift!

Special Limited-time Offer

Mail to Silhouette Reader Service™

3010 Walden Avenue
P.O. Box 1867
Buffalo, N.Y. 14269-1867

YES! Please send me 4 free Silhouette Desire® novels and my free surprise gift. Then send me 6 brand-new novels every month, which I will receive months before they appear in bookstores. Bill me at the low price of $2.44 each plus 25¢ delivery and applicable sales tax, if any.* That's the complete price and—compared to the cover prices of $2.99 each—quite a bargain! I understand that accepting the books and gift places me under no obligation ever to buy any books. I can always return a shipment and cancel at any time. Even if I never buy another book from Silhouette, the 4 free books and the surprise gift are mine to keep forever.

225 BPA ANRS

Name	(PLEASE PRINT)	
Address		Apt. No.
City	State	Zip

UDES-94R   ©1990 Harlequin Enterprises Limited

It's our 1000th Silhouette Romance, and we're celebrating!

Join us for a special collection of love stories by authors you've loved for years, and new favorites you've just discovered. Join the celebration...

April
REGAN'S PRIDE by **Diana Palmer**
MARRY ME AGAIN by **Suzanne Carey**

May
THE BEST IS YET TO BE by **Tracy Sinclair**
CAUTION: BABY AHEAD by **Marie Ferrarella**

June
THE BACHELOR PRINCE by **Debbie Macomber**
A ROGUE'S HEART by **Laurie Paige**

July
IMPROMPTU BRIDE by **Annette Broadrick**
THE FORGOTTEN HUSBAND by **Elizabeth August**

Silhouette Romance...vibrant, fun and emotionally rich! Take another look at us! And as part of the celebration, readers can receive a FREE gift!

You'll fall in love all over
again with
Silhouette Romance!

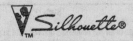

CEL1000

SILHOUETTE®

Desire®

Centerfold™

They're sexy, they're determined, they're trouble with a capital *T!*

Meet six of the steamiest, most stubborn heroes you'd ever want to know, and learn *everything* about them....

August's *Man of the Month,* Quinn Donovan, in **FUSION** by Cait London

Mr. Bad Timing, Dan Kingman, in **DREAMS AND SCHEMES** by Merline Lovelace

Mr. Marriage-phobic, Connor Devlin, in **WHAT ARE FRIENDS FOR?** by Naomi Horton

Mr. Sensible, Lucas McCall, in **HOT PROPERTY** by Rita Rainville

Mr. Know-it-all, Thomas Kane, in **NIGHTFIRE** by Barbara McCauley

Mr. Macho, Jake Powers, in **LOVE POWER** by Susan Carroll

Look for them on the covers so you can see just how handsome and irresistible they are!

Coming in August only from Silhouette Desire!

**Rugged and lean...and the best-looking,
sweetest-talking men to be found in the
entire Lone Star state!**

*Diana
Palmer*

LONG, TALL
TEXANS

In July 1994, Silhouette is very proud to bring you
Diana Palmer's first three LONG, TALL TEXANS.
CALHOUN, JUSTIN and TYLER—the three cowboys
who started the legend. Now they're back by popular
demand in one classic volume—and they're ready to
lasso your heart! Beautifully repackaged for this
special event, this collection is sure to be a
longtime keepsake!

"Diana Palmer makes a reader want to find a Texan
of her own to love!"   —*Affaire de Coeur*

**LONG, TALL TEXANS—the first three—
reunited in this special roundup!**

**Available in July,
wherever Silhouette books are sold.**

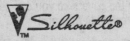

Silhouette®

LTT